MURDER OF PEARL

MURDER OF PEARL

A SILVERMAN SISTERS COZY MYSTERY

PEARL PARTY COZY MYSTERIES
BOOK ONE

NELLIE H. STEELE

For Kelly and Jodi, who inspired this series

CHARACTER LIST

Pearl Willow Barlow – The owner of Willow Lake Estate and matriarch of the Barlow family.

Melissa Barlow – Pearl's daughter

Abby Barton – Melissa's college friend who recently returned from Greece

Harper Martin – Melissa's college friend

Emily Collins – Pearl's sister-in-law

Madison Montgomery – Melissa's college friend

Penelope Collins – Emily's daughter and Pearl's niece

Aurora Powell – Melissa's college friend

Everly Dixon – Melissa's college roommate

Addison Newton – Pearl's brother's daughter

Willow Olsen – Pearl's sister's daughter

Reagan Walker – Pearl's cousin

Aubrey Robinson – Pearl's second cousin and Reagan's daughter

Kennedy Moore – Pearl's attorney

Peyton Carter – Pearl's cousin-in-law

Julia Palmer – Pearl's sister

Parker Neal – Pearl's brother's daughter

CHAPTER 1

Kelly shoved the knife further into the slit, hitting flesh and tearing it. She grimaced with effort and her nose scrunched at the smell. Liquid oozed out onto her gloved hands, sopping the towel she'd placed underneath for the mess.

I'm gonna gut you like yesterday's catch, she thought.

Aloud, she exclaimed, "Oh, this is a tough one! Come on, you!"

She glanced up at the camera and offered a tentative smile. The knife finally did its work. The top of the oyster popped off.

"There we go," Kelly said, once again glancing at the camera. "And, oh my gosh, you guys, this one is so beautiful!"

She whisked the pearl off into a bowl of salt off-camera to clean it, then smiled at the camera. "Who's excited to see this pearl?"

Bright lights glared down on her within her make-shift basement studio. Two large umbrella lights shone from either side. With her laptop perched on a stand and her cell phone also connected to read comments, Kelly shifted her eyes between each screen, switching back and forth between scanning for comments and making eye contact with the camera.

Across the room, her younger sister, Jodi, monitored her orders page. She held up two fingers and wiggled them at Kelly. Kelly gave a slight nod to acknowledge the additional two orders received as she shifted the pearl from the salt bowl to the water bowl.

She offered the camera another smile, and arched her eyebrow as she swept the pearl under the cover of a towel to dry it before its reveal. After years with the Pearls Unlimited company, a business specializing in pearl-set jewelry, she'd become a master at all things pearl party-related.

Together with Jodi, Kelly worked to organize events like in-home or online pearl parties as part of their sales plan. Customers placed an order for jewelry, and with each piece, they received a live oyster opening.

Kelly would shuck an oyster, remove its pearl, and then measure and show its color to the purchaser, before the pearl was set into the jewelry of their choice. The draw was the allure and mystery surrounding which size and color of pearl the purchaser would receive.

Off-camera, Kelly set the pearl on a display card before sliding it in front of the lens. With her "pearl-vision" lens slid into place, Kelly held the pearl in front of the special set-up.

"Ladies, this is an absolutely gorgeous rose pink. And it looks like at least a size seven. Melanie, girl, you are lucky with this one."

Messages scrolled up her screen as party viewers extolled the virtues of the beautiful, rich-colored pearl. After showcasing the pearl, Kelly measured it before sliding it into an envelope marked with Melanie's name. She gave the group an overview of the jewelry piece Melanie had selected, showing them a picture of the necklace in her catalog.

After she revealed the rose-colored pearl, three more orders popped on the screen. Jodi wiggled three fingers at Kelly.

"All right, ladies, keep those orders coming. I'm here until they stop. And remember, no more parties for another two weeks after this one! Jodi and I are booked for an exclusive private event this coming weekend!

"I'll have plenty of pictures when I get back to share with you *and* one lucky gal will win access to our next still-to-be-determined weekend event at the end of the party tonight! All you have to do to be entered is place an order."

Kelly recited the order information off by heart as Jodi posted instructions in the live stream video's chat.

She powered through the remainder of the party, opening over thirty oysters before the party concluded. She wound down with another promise of pictures from the exclusive weekend event, a wink, and a wave.

As the camera's light blinked off, Kelly blew out a long breath.

"Well, that was a whopper of a party," she said to Jodi, as she slumped in her chair. She fanned herself with her hands. "Gosh, these lights are hot."

"Getting you ready for the spotlight this weekend."

Kelly sucked in a breath as she leaned forward and started to clean up the soppy towel soaked with smelly oyster juice. "How many oyster openings do we have for that one so far?"

Jodi shuffled through a stack of papers. "One hundred twenty-two."

Kelly dropped the drenched towel onto the tabletop. Her eyebrows shot toward her hairline.

"What?!" she exclaimed, eyes wide.

"And more to come, probably," Jodi said. "I told you before, this one was a fantastic setting. Old mansion, lots of ladies with disposable income."

"What's the occasion again?"

"Someone named Pearl's birthday. One of her friends or something thought it would be a cute theme to have a pearl-themed party for Pearl."

"And we're the only 'entertainment,' so to speak?" Kelly asked, as she continued her clean-up.

"That was my understanding," Jodi answered. "They want a jewelry showcase on Friday, pearl openings on Saturday afternoon, and a pearl-themed cocktail party Saturday night. We don't have to do anything to prepare for that, but we were invited. And then Sunday brunch followed by openings for any last-minute orders."

Kelly blinked her eyelids rapidly as she considered the whirlwind weekend ahead.

Jodi reached out and clapped a hand on Kelly's shoulder. "Relax, Kelly, it'll be fun."

"What I can't understand," Kelly answered, as she stuffed a wad of wet paper towels into her trashcan, "is why women with enough money to rent out this mansion for the weekend for someone's birthday party hired us to provide the entertainment? Come on – they must have much more extravagant jewelry than what we offer."

"They didn't rent out the house," Jodi answered. "It's Pearl's place."

"Wait, I thought this was in a B&B or one of those murder mystery mansions or whatever?"

"Nope. Willow Lake Estate belongs to Pearl."

Kelly widened her eyes again. "Now, I *really* don't understand why they hired us."

"Who cares? We'll probably do over one-hundred and

fifty openings over the weekend, and if we're lucky, we'll get a few more bookings. Plus, it's all expenses paid! They provide the rooms, food, everything."

"I guess it's not a bad way to spend a weekend."

Jodi grinned. "It's going to be a killer weekend."

CHAPTER 2

Kelly leaned forward, closing the gap between her and the windshield. Her white knuckles gripped the steering wheel as she squinted to find the road.

Her windshield wipers fought to swish the rain from her soaked windshield. She blinked her eyes repeatedly, as though that would help clear her vision. Her tires splashed through another puddle, sending a spray of water high into the air.

"Ugh," Kelly groaned, as rain pounded against their small car's roof.

"You should have bought that crossover SUV," Jodi mumbled from the passenger's seat.

"If you can't say anything helpful, pipe down, Jodi," Kelly warned.

They drove for another few moments before Kelly groaned again. "This weather is terrible! I can barely see the road!"

"It's not much further," Jodi said.

"Thank goodness. My wipers are losing the battle against the torrential downpour."

Jodi let out a sigh as she studied the passing scenery. "Once we get there, we can park the car and enjoy the weekend."

"IF we get there," Kelly huffed. "This weekend is starting off terribly!"

"We'll make it," Jodi countered. "I told you, it's not much further!"

Kelly crawled along the slick road as the rain buffeted the car. Her windshield wipers, set on high, flicked back and forth wildly, but the path ahead resembled a melted painting as the rain fell in torrents.

Moments later, the skies offered another assault. Chunks of hail pounded down around them.

"Oh!" Kelly exclaimed, as the sound threatened to drown out her own thoughts. "You've *got* to be kidding!"

"What?!" Jodi shouted over the din.

"I SAID YOU'VE GOT TO BE KIDDING!" Kelly yelled back, as the marble-sized chunks pounded their roof and the road around them.

"Look on the bright side," Jodi said, her voice still at a holler. "Soon we'll be at a mansion!"

Kelly tightened her grip on the steering wheel again and leaned forward, narrowing her eyes at the road. Another few nerve-wracking minutes passed before the hail let up, and a few more drops of rain fell before the precipitation ceased entirely.

"There!" Jodi said, waving her hand at the clearing weather.

Kelly shot a narrow-eyed glance in her direction, a silent response designed to pass along her annoyance without a word.

"I hope it lasts long enough to get the luggage in," Kelly said after a moment.

Jodi fiddled with her phone in the passenger's seat.

"Will you stop playing with that phone and help me figure out where we're going?" Kelly said.

"I'm fiddling with the phone so I can tell you where to go," Jodi answered. "Oh, there." She waved a finger out the window.

"Where?" Kelly asked.

"There." Jodi pointed to a small road, hidden by the leaves of a large and sagging tree. Kelly passed the road, unable to make the turn given the short notice. "You missed it."

"You didn't tell me until the last second!"

"I told you way before!" Jodi countered.

"No, you didn't," Kelly said, hunting for a place to turn around.

"Yes, I did. I said there forever ago. You were too busy complaining about me using my phone."

"What, that vague "meh" thing you did? I had no idea what you were even talking about."

"Just find a place to turn around and go back."

"Yeah, I'm trying. Do you see any suitable locations? The roads are half-washed out from that rainstorm. I'm not going to try to inch onto the shoulder. We'll get stuck."

"If you would have bought that crossover…"

"Don't even say it," Kelly shot back through clenched teeth.

With a huff, Kelly adjusted her grip on the steering wheel as she frowned, detecting the subtle eyeballing from Jodi at the last statement. She found another side road and, after completing a three-way turn, headed back in the direction they'd come.

"It's up here on the left," Jodi announced, as the road came into view. "Enough time for you?"

"Yes, thank you," Kelly retorted, flicking on her turn signal and easing the car onto the small side road. They rounded a bend, and the house came into view. Rising high on a hill, the gothic-style mansion with its dark, rambling roof, multiple chimneys, and massive facade contrasted the gray sky behind it.

Kelly gulped as she ducked to stare up at it. "Yikes, looks like something out of a horror movie."

"It does not," Jodi argued. "I can't imagine what it would be like to live there. It's huge!"

"Good, we'll have plenty of places to hide from the crazed murderer then. Or the ghosts."

Kelly continued toward the house, making no additional mistakes given the obvious path forward. She pulled up to a set of black iron gates. Two large, brick columns stood on either side. The fence stretched as far as she could see around the property. A communication port rose from a thin, silver rod at the side of the entrance.

Kelly pressed the large silver button. A buzzing sounded. Kelly glanced at the large gate, expecting it to open. She threw her hands in the air as nothing happened, and pressed the button again.

A camera on one of the red brick pillars rotated down slightly, before a tinny voice sounded from the speaker next to the button.

"Yes?" a clipped male's voice answered.

"Ah, hi," Kelly said, leaning out the window and pressing the button as she spoke.

A garbled response came back. She let off the button before pressing it again. "What?" she questioned.

"Ma'am," the voice said.

"Yes?" Kelly inquired, pressing the button as she spoke.

"Ma'am, please stop pressing the button when you're speaking. I can't hear you."

"Oh, sorry," Kelly said, feeling color rising in her cheeks. She shot Jodi a glance as she fidgeted in her seat.

"Can I help you?" the voice responded.

"Yes, I need the gate opened."

No one responded for several moments. Kelly stared at the small silver box. She screwed up her face and shrugged.

"Name?" the voice finally responded.

"Oh, ah, Kelly Silverman."

"And Jodi!" Jodi shouted.

"Yes, and Jodi Silverman. We're together. The Silverman sisters!"

With no further verbal response, a buzzing suddenly sounded, and the gates began to slowly crawl open.

"Oh!" Kelly quickly shifted from park to drive. "THANK YOU!" she shouted, as she pulled through the gates.

The long winding drive, lined with large pine trees, hid the house from view at times. The paved driveway's incline turned steep. Kelly pressed her accelerator closer to the floor, urging her little car up the steep hill. The trees cleared at the top, revealing a large circular drive leading to the front door on the opposite side of a massive stone fountain.

Water spit from various gargoyle's mouths perched on a raised platform. Below them, three women stood with their backs to each other. With robes wrapped around them, they clutched their midriffs with one hand and covered their eyes with the other, their heads hanging in sadness.

Kelly winced at it as they circled it. "Well, that's creepy," she muttered.

"It's not that bad. It's very… artistic," Jodi said.

Kelly shot her a glance. "You're reaching. That's horrible. They look sad. Who would want that in front of their house? Just because it's big and ostentatious doesn't mean it's art."

Kelly eased the car to a stop and threw the shifter into park. After pulling on the emergency brake, she ducked to glance up at the large structure looming over them.

With her foot, she kicked open her car door and stepped

out. She spun to study the house, shielding her eyes from the sunshine peeking through the gray clouds.

Her nose wrinkled and a sour expression formed on her lips. The stone, darkened in several places by dirt and age, rose high in the sky, topped by a peaked roof. The building sprawled in both directions from the centrally placed door. Gargoyles perched on the roof's edge.

Jodi climbed from the car and popped open the trunk, unloading her luggage.

"Wait!" Kelly called, waving her hand in the air. She hurried to Jodi's side and stuffed her suitcase back in the trunk.

"What are you doing?" Jodi demanded.

"We're not staying here."

"What?"

"It's creepy! I've got a terrible, terrible feeling. Let's just go. We'll say we got sick or something. Family emergency, anything. Let's just get out of here."

Jodi pulled her suitcase out of the trunk a second time and placed it on the ground. "You're being ridiculous."

She pulled another bag from the trunk and shouldered it.

Kelly tossed the suitcase back inside the trunk again. "I'm not! Look at this place! There are creatures looming on the roof, and the strange fountain, and the creepy mansion. The whole thing is weirding me out. I have a bad feeling."

CHAPTER 3

$\mathcal{J}$odi rolled her eyes and pulled her luggage from the trunk again. "You can do what you want. I'm staying. When will we ever get the chance to stay in a place like this again? I'll bet the inside is amazing!"

"Hello, ladies!" another woman's voice said, joining the conversation.

"Too late to back out now!" Jodi whispered with a smile, as she pulled another bag from the trunk. She twisted to face the house, her smile broadening. "Hi!"

A smartly dressed woman approached, leaving the front door open behind her. She teetered on her spiked red heels. Diagonal gold stripes ran over teal fabric to form breezy pants, topped with a rust-red colored blouse decorated with tiny navy-blue horses and a pussycat bow.

Jodi stuck her hand out as the woman strutted over to them. "I'm Jodi, and this is my sister, Kelly." Jodi thumbed toward Kelly.

"Melissa Barlow," the woman said, as she swept a lock of platinum blonde hair over her shoulder and shook Jodi's hand. "I'm Pearl's daughter, and the one who booked you for the party."

"Oh, we spoke a few times on the phone, then," Jodi answered, with a nod.

Melissa eyed Kelly head to toe as she offered her hand. "Hi," Kelly said, with a lopsided smile. "I'm Kelly. I'm the one who actually does the work."

Melissa raised her eyebrows at the statement.

"Of opening the oysters, I mean. Jodi won't touch them." Kelly stuck her tongue out and made a face like she was gagging. "She thinks they're gross." She gave a nervous chuckle, before adding, "Jodi does bugs though. I don't do bugs. Jodi gets those."

She giggled again, clasping her hands in front of her.

Melissa stood speechless in front of them as though she was stunned by the story Kelly babbled to her. After a moment, she waved her hand in the air like she was clearing it and said, "Ah, well, great. Welcome to Willow Lake Estate. I can show you to your rooms if you'd like to dump your bags and … " she paused as she eyed Kelly again, "change."

Kelly scrunched her face at the statement, as she glanced down at her casual attire, consisting of a pair of leggings and a cozy tunic.

"Great!" Jodi said, grasping the handle of her suitcase and pulling it along behind her. She lifted her makeup case from the trunk as she walked with Melissa to the front entrance.

Kelly's jaw dropped as she stared at the remaining pieces of luggage in the trunk. Along with her suitcase and makeup bag, she had all the pearl party supplies. With a roll of her eyes, she slung one bag over her head, letting it fall to her right hip. She crossed another over the opposite way and it landed against her left hip. She hoisted her makeup case as far up her arm as she could before tugging the handle of the wheeled suitcase upward.

She swung the trunk shut before she grabbed the suitcase and dragged it with her toward the door. As she took her first step, the wheel on her suitcase cracked. Broken pieces skittered across the driveway.

Kelly shut her eyes in disgust and frustration. "You've *got* to be kidding me." With a silent prayer for patience, Kelly grasped the leather handle on the top and hefted it up. She began a slow waddle toward the door.

Melissa stuck her head outside. "Yoo-hoo! Coming?"

"Yep," Kelly wheezed. "Just grabbing all the luggage."

"Great!" The well-dressed woman ducked back inside, leaving Kelly to continue her slow toddle toward the entrance.

She struggled through the open doorway, banging three of the four bags off the door frame as she side-stepped her way into the foyer.

"There you are!" Jodi exclaimed. "Isn't this place great?"

"Sorry, my wheel broke," Kelly said as she sucked in air, setting the lopsided luggage down on the dark patterned marble floor.

She scanned the massive space, biting her lower lip. Large windows let light into the dark area, but still failed to brighten it. Enormous blood-red pillars rose to the ceiling several stories higher than them. Large doors closed off several other rooms, branching off from the foyer.

A wide staircase with more stairs than Kelly wished to count climbed to another floor. At the top of the stairs stood a painting, twice life-sized, of a stern, blond-haired woman. She clutched a cane, her jaw set, her eyes slightly narrowed. With her lifted chin, she appeared to be glaring down at anyone in the foyer. Massive strands of pearls hung around her neck.

Two large bronze lions sat at each side of the staircase, silent sentinels studying anyone who passed between them.

Their mouths hung open, frozen in an endless roar. One front paw on each extended out toward the stairs, the massive feet stretched open with razor-sharp claws bared.

Kelly swallowed hard as she frowned at the threatening beasts. Jodi seemed to ignore them entirely as her eyes floated around the space, a grin on her lips.

"This place is amazing!" she said to Melissa. "I can't imagine growing up here!"

Melissa lifted a shoulder in nonchalance as they continued to survey the space. "You're welcome to look around after I've shown you to your rooms. Anything locked is obviously off-limits, and please keep your roaming to the main floor, since the second has occupied bedrooms."

Jodi gave her a giddy smile and a nod. "Well, lead away! I can't wait to see my bedroom!" She gushed as she hurried to the staircase, seeming oblivious to the bronze threats on either side.

"Jodi!" Kelly exclaimed.

"What?" Jodi hissed, as she spun to face Kelly.

"A little help?" Kelly said, shrugging to wiggle the bags at her hips.

With a roll of her eyes, Jodi stomped across the marble floor, the heels of her high-heeled boots clicking across the stone and her long necklaces swinging with every step. She yanked Kelly's small makeup case from her forearm and crossed back to Melissa, who waited at the steps.

Kelly's shoulders slumped at the underwhelming "help." With a roll of her eyes, she shuffled across the ornate floor, dragging her damaged suitcase behind her. It wobbled back and forth as it struggled to stay on one wheel.

With a sigh, she shoved the extendable handle back into the suitcase and lifted it by the leather strap as she stepped onto the first stair. Kelly's eyes floated up to the portrait of the older woman. She fluttered her eyelashes at the many steps between her and the massive painting. A wide landing led to a steeper and longer set of stairs. Her eyes roamed up the many steps, taking a mental inventory. She lost count after twenty.

Jodi, already halfway to the top, chattered away to Melissa, who managed to scale the mountainous stairway with ease despite her four-inch heels.

Even in her flat athletic shoes, Kelly gave a preemptive groan, before beginning her ascent. She scrunched her nose and hurried past the lions. Halfway up, she took a break, puffing a few breaths before she continued her climb.

Two more lions awaited her as she reached the top. With a shake of her head, she hurried to the left, trying to catch up with Jodi and Melissa. They wound through a series of hallways. Melissa finally came to a stop outside two massive wooden doors.

Kelly pitied the person who had to dust the intricate details on each. Melissa grasped hold of a large doorknob, a roaring lion's face imprinted on it, and swung the door open.

"Jodi, this is your room. Kelly, yours is the next set of doors. The rooms connected through a shared bathroom."

Jodi's eyes lit up as she stepped through the door. "Oh, wow!" she exclaimed. "Thank you! This is amazing."

Melissa gave her a curt nod and a puckered smile as Kelly lumbered through the door, struggling with the three bags.

"Dinner is at six-thirty," Melissa called in from the hall, as Jodi wandered around in the room. "Smart casual dress." She eyed Kelly again as she said this. "Cocktails beginning at six. Most of the gals should be here by then, so you can meet everyone."

"Sounds great!" Jodi called.

Kelly dropped her suitcase and began to peel the bags off with a groan. She kicked the door shut as she heard Melissa's footsteps pound down the hall, muffled only by the thick runner.

With another sigh, Kelly collapsed onto the massive king-sized bed across from the door. Jodi leapt from the bed just as Kelly sat down. She twirled in the room, her hands thrown out to her sides. She let her head drop back between her shoulders.

"Isn't this *marvelous*?" she asked, a broad grin on her face as she snapped her head up to stare at Kelly.

Kelly wore a shocked expression on her face. She gave a slight shake to her head as her eyes flitted over the room's features. "Ah, in a word, no."

Jodi screwed up her face. "Are you kidding me? *Look* at this room!" Her hands formed fists and she jiggled them with excitement.

"This room is creepy. This entire house is creepy."

"What? You're kidding? This place is amazing! I can't wait to explore. Hurry up and dump your stuff in your room so we can go look around."

"I don't think I want to look around. I want to leave. This place is spooky. Did you see those giant lions at the top and bottom of the stairs?"

"Yeah, aren't they great? You've *got* to get a picture of me with them!"

"And then this room. First, the roaring lion doorknob and then…" Kelly scrunched up her nose and waved her hand around.

"What?" Jodi asked, her shoulders slumping. She let her eyes travel over the space as if she searched for Kelly's meaning.

Kelly's eyes widened. "You can't be serious?" Kelly questioned.

Jodi lifted a shoulder and gave Kelly a quizzical look.

Kelly set her mouth in a line, her shoulders dropping an

inch before she replied. She closed her eyes for a moment, then fluttered them open and responded, "The whole creepy baby thing. Come on, you can't actually think it's not creepy."

Jodi focused on the wooden carvings gracing the corners of the room. "The angels?"

"Those aren't angels. They're creepy little babies, staring at your bed from every corner."

"They're not babies. They're not that bad."

Kelly shook her head and pushed herself to stand. "I hope they aren't in my room."

Jodi grabbed her broken suitcase and dragged it toward the shared bathroom. Kelly lifted one of the other bags containing the pearl party paraphernalia and followed her.

She pushed open the door to the massive bathroom separating their rooms.

"Oh, wow!" Jodi exclaimed, running a finger over the claw-footed tub in the middle of the space. "I would LOVE to soak in this."

"I am not sitting naked in water in this house, no way," Kelly said, as she continued through the bathroom.

They pushed into Kelly's room, which was decorated in heavy woods and sapphire blue linens.

"Whew, no creepy babies," Kelly murmured, as she scanned the trim.

"There, happy? Now, hurry up and change so we can explore."

Kelly flung her suitcase onto a luggage rack in the room and spun to face Jodi. "I am not running around this huge house in anything but my tennies." She tilted her foot toward Jodi to show off her white Superga sneakers.

Jodi opened her mouth to argue, when Kelly waved her hands in front of her. "I will change before the party tonight. But I'm not running around the house in some ridiculous outfit. My knees will be killing me."

"Suit yourself. I'm going in this!"

"Fine by me. If you want to traipse around in those heels, that's your business."

The grin returned to Jodi's face, and she let out an excited squeak. "Let's go!"

She grabbed Kelly's hand and tugged her to the large double doors leading to the hall. They padded down the wide hallway on the thick red runner before reaching a branch. Jodi looked both ways as though she was about to cross a busy street, before she pointed to her right. "This way, I think."

They wound through several hallways upstairs, backtracking a few times, before they found their way to the main staircase. Jodi skipped down the steps while Kelly stamped her way down to the bottom.

"Take a picture of me with the lion!" Jodi requested. She stood on the ball of one foot, a hand on her hip, the other arm wrapped around the lion's neck.

Kelly held back a sigh as she lined up her shot with her iPhone and snapped a picture.

"One more!" Jodi said. She extended her fingers like the lion's paw and snarled. Kelly snapped another picture before they moved on.

They spent another two hours exploring the main floor of the house.

A large sitting room stood off the main foyer. The fireplace, a foot taller than Kelly and nearly ten feet across, boasted two life-sized lion statues on each side. The massive bronze beasts stood on all fours, crouched in a strike position, a snarl frozen on their lips.

A grand piano tucked into the corner of the room appeared tiny compared to the size of the space.

"Wow," Jodi whispered, her voice echoing in the room. "Can you imagine this being your living room?"

"Can you imagine how much wood it must take to keep a fire going?" Kelly eyed the lions again. "These people love lions."

"Come on, let's keep going."

An enormous greenhouse area contained an indoor rose garden and a few flowering trees which neither of them could identify. A fountain sat at the center of the space. In the fountain's center, a woman screamed in apparent terror at some unknown threat as water cascaded over her.

"What's with all the creepy lady fountains?" Kelly asked, frowning at it.

"Dunno," Jodi mumbled, as she smelled a few of the roses. "Should we move on?"

"Definitely," Kelly said, still frowning at the creepy fountain.

They continued to navigate through the floor plan, finding a flowing stream outside the greenhouse, leading down a hall. Steppingstones dotted the moving water every few feet to allow people to traverse the hall without becoming wet.

They hopped from stone to stone as they studied the stream.

"How is this water moving?" Kelly inquired.

"Must be on some kind of system, like a lazy river," Jodi suggested, as she balanced on one stone before leaping to the next.

"They should put ducks in here and you can play pick-a-duck like at the amusement park."

The comment elicited a chuckle from Jodi as they reached the end and stepped onto dry ground.

"What's through those doors?" Jodi asked, pointing to a set of iron doors. Two large carousel horses decorated each door.

"Creepy playroom?" Kelly ventured.

"Let's find out." Jodi stalked forward and grabbed one of the giant handles, styled like a carousel pole. "Help me." She glanced over her shoulder at Kelly as she pointed to the other handle.

Kelly braced herself as she grabbed hold of the massive handle and tugged. With some effort, they inched the doors backward. A grinding noise sounded, and a hidden mechanism whirred. Music filled the air. Warm light flickered before glowing to life, illuminating the space.

Kelly's eyes went wide, and her jaw dropped open. Jodi wore a similar expression.

"OMG," Kelly whispered, as she eyed the room's contents.

A grin formed on Jodi's lips, and she glanced at Kelly.

"Come on!" She grabbed Kelly's hand and pulled her toward the room.

They stopped before entering, preparing themselves for stepping onto the spinning platform. In front of them, carousel horses bobbed up and down, while a calliope belted out a perky tune.

Jodi let go of Kelly's hand and stepped onto the platform, spreading her legs and arms out to steady herself. "Come on!" she shouted again.

Kelly pushed a lock of hair behind her ear as Jodi circled away from her and bit her lower lip. She studied the floor's spiraling motion before she hopped over the edge and onto the spinning platform.

She wavered back and forth as she fought to stay upright on her feet. Jodi giggled as she slipped her feet into the stirrup of a chestnut-colored horse and swung her leg over the top. Kelly climbed atop a snow-white horse, its head tossed back in a whinny.

"I can't believe they have a carousel in the house! Who has a working carousel?" Kelly shouted as they spun around.

Jodi kicked her legs out as she clutched her horse's reins. "I can't believe we get to stay here!"

They rode the carousel for another ten minutes before they climbed off the horses and hopped off the platform, pushing the doors closed behind them. They continued down the hall in a cloud of giggles.

"Okay," Kelly said, her arm threaded through Jodi's, "I'll admit that was fun."

"No kidding. Who has a carousel room?"

"Besides that Hugh Crain guy in The Haunting, I don't know," Kelly said.

"Not even he had horses," Jodi corrected. "They just had a room that spun."

"The horses were a nice touch, I'll admit."

They continued down the hall to the foyer, discussing the other oddities in the house. As they spilled into the massive entryway, their conversation and laughter ground to a halt. A skinny rail of a woman stood dead center in the room. She clutched a cane and stood stick straight.

Kelly recognized her immediately as the woman in the oversized painting at the top of the stairs.

"Oh!" Kelly exclaimed, sobering quickly. "Hi." She swallowed hard as the woman's gaze traveled up and down her form, before she set her mouth in a firm line, corners turning down.

CHAPTER 4

"*A*h, hello," Kelly repeated. "I'm Kelly Silverman, and this is my sister, Jodi. I'm…"

"Yes, I know who you are," the older woman answered. "The pearl people." She spat out the words as though the idea disgusted her.

"Right," Kelly said. "We're from Pearls Unlimited. Are you Pearl? We're here to provide some fun for your birthday! Happy birthday!"

The woman gave them an unimpressed glance. "Yes, I am Pearl Willow Barlow. Melissa hired you, not me. I have no desire to see the pearl pulled from within the oyster."

"It can be really fun!" Kelly offered. "Waiting to see the color you'll get and figuring out which setting you want to place it in."

Pearl arched a gray eyebrow at her. "Just try not to ruin the linens."

She spun to depart, when Kelly called, "Oh, by the way, we just found the carousel room. We had a blast in there. I can't imagine having a carousel in your house!"

Pearl studied the pair of them up and down again before

narrowing her eyes. "Yes, I imagine you would find that amusing."

She twisted away from them again and disappeared down the hall, the rapping of her cane announcing every step she took.

Overhead, thunder rumbled and lightning flashed, illuminating the space briefly through the floor-to-ceiling windows at the top of the stairs.

"Well, she was pleasant," Kelly said, her voice dripping in sarcasm.

Jodi winced and side-eyed Kelly. "Melissa seems excited," she said with a shrug.

Another blast of thunder boomed overhead. Kelly's eyes slid skyward. "I'm not sure I'm going to enjoy being in this house during a storm."

"Well, get used to it. The forecast calls for a stormy weekend."

Kelly frowned. "I guess we'd better get ready for the party."

"Put on your happy face – it's almost showtime!" Jodi said.

They made their way back upstairs, finding Melissa milling around outside of their rooms.

"Ah, there you are!" she exclaimed.

"Sorry, we were exploring," Kelly explained.

Melissa gave her a curt smile. "The reason I was looking for you was to ask if you could do a mini-party tonight? Maybe before dinner? Just to showcase the process and show off a few pearls. Maybe we can do a flash sale; the first five women who order get these oysters, or something. You're the expert – whatever you think." She waved her hands at Kelly.

"Oh, um…" Kelly hesitated.

"She'd be happy to!" Jodi exclaimed.

Kelly glanced at her and offered a smile as she hid a huff behind a laugh. "Well, I need to set a few things up–"

"Oh, absolutely! You should still have time before you–" she paused, eyeing Kelly's comfy clothes again, "change." Her voice dripped with disdain. She cocked her head and continued. "You can set up in the sitting room. I had a table put out for you near the fireplace."

"The one with the massive lions?"

"That's the one!" Melissa exclaimed, flicking her finger in the air. "Thanks, ladies. See you at six-thirty!"

Kelly smiled at the woman as she disappeared down the hall. With a sigh, she said, "We better get moving if we're going to set up for this."

"And change," Jodi said, eyeing Kelly up and down and doing her best impression of Melissa.

"Don't remind me," Kelly grumbled. "Come on."

They spent forty-five minutes laying out their materials on the table in the enormous sitting room. Kelly set up her salt and water bowls, padded the table with extra towels, and put out her shucking board, knife and bucket of oysters.

Jodi placed a few pieces of jewelry on each side of the table and dropped several catalogs around the room.

"That should do it," Jodi said, as she scanned the decorated space. "We'd better get going and change. We don't have much time!"

Kelly nodded in agreement, and they hurried up the long staircase and wound through the halls to their bedrooms.

Kelly unzipped her suitcase and pawed through the clothes she'd packed, suddenly feeling as though everything was inadequate. She found her dress for the evening and laid it out on the bed, desperately trying to flatten it to remove any wrinkles.

She glanced in the full-length mirror and winced. The trek through the castle had taken a bigger toll than she'd expected. Her hair stuck out at wild angles and her makeup was smudged.

She dug through her makeup bag and quickly fixed her face. She found a pearl-studded hair clip and swept her hair to one side.

A check of the time showed she had minutes to finish changing. She ripped off her clothes, tossing them on the bed to deal with later. She tugged on the navy sweater dress, wishing she'd brought something fancier. Hopping around on one foot, she tugged on one gray suede boot, then the other. A bead of sweat formed on her brow as she collapsed on the bed and zipped up the flat boots.

She blew out a long breath as she stood and adjusted her dress.

"Ready?" Jodi asked from the doorway leading to the bathroom.

"Yep," Kelly said, still tugging at the dress.

Jodi scrunched her nose. "That's what you brought for the cocktail party?"

"What?" Kelly asked, glancing down at it. She eyed Jodi's outfit. In a gold-foil halter dress that fell to her knees and matching spiked heels with an ankle strap, Jodi looked dressed to the nines. Large gold hoops nearly grazed her shoulders, on full display since she'd pulled up her hair into a chic French twist.

Kelly narrowed her eyes. "Where did you get that?"

"What?" Jodi inquired, playing dumb.

"That dress," Kelly said, as though it was obvious.

"Oh, uh," Jodi mumbled, screwing up her face and shrugging a shoulder. "I found it on a clearance rack somewhere."

Kelly gave her an unimpressed glance.

"I may have another one if you want to borrow it."

"That you also found on the clearance rack?"

"Uh, yep. I was going to return it, but you can have it.

Hurry up, we're going to be late!" Jodi said, as she hurried through the bathroom. "And take off those horrible boots."

"What's wrong with these boots? I like these boots."

"They're great for a weekend mall run. Not a cocktail party at Willow Lake Estate."

"Remember I have to shuck in this," Kelly answered.

Jodi waved her comment away and rummaged through her suitcase, while Kelly pulled off her boots. Jodi pulled a silver-lilac dress with a lace overlay from the suitcase and tossed it to Kelly. Kelly shimmied out of her sweater dress and into the knee-length, cap-sleeve dress.

Jodi set out a pair of silver peep-toe t-straps. "Good thing we're the same size."

"Ugh, I hate heels," Kelly groaned, as she squeezed her foot into the shoe and buckled it.

"Hurry up," Jodi implored.

"Okay, okay," Kelly said, buckling her second shoe and standing on wobbly legs. "Just give me a second to get my sea legs."

Thunder rumbled overhead again. Wind whipped outside the window, blowing the trees wildly.

"Sounds like another storm," Kelly said, as she hobbled to the door.

"Yeah," Jodi agreed. "Thank goodness we don't have to drive!"

Rain pounded against the massive windows above the main staircase. Kelly glanced up at the skylight. Black clouds rolled across the sky and lightning pulsed. Large droplets of rain bombarded the glass.

With a firm grip on the banister, Kelly tottered down the stairs. She adjusted the skirt of her dress and smoothed her hair when she reached the bottom.

"Come on!" Jodi grumbled through clenched teeth, as she waited across the foyer. Kelly tiptoed across the floor in an awkward half-run, half-crawl. "Careful with those shoes!"

Kelly cleared her throat as she smoothed her dress again. "Okay, let's go," she said as she caught up with Jodi.

Jodi spun and plastered a smile on her face. They wandered into the massive sitting room through the open doors. Melissa stood with a half-empty champagne flute in her hand, surrounded by four other women. Melissa, an animated expression on her face, waved her hand in the air as she chattered away. After a moment, they all burst into cackling laughter. Other women milled around the room in pairs or trios. A few glanced at Kelly's setup or flipped through one of the catalogs.

Kelly arched an eyebrow at the scene. "This looks like mean-girl central."

She shot a glance at Jodi, who appeared to actually be enjoying the spectacle. Melissa waved at them and approached, leaving her posse behind.

"There you are!" she said, as she narrowed the gap between them. "You two clean up nicely. And here I worried you'd come in something like a sweater dress." She issued the high-pitched cackle again.

Kelly offered a gratuitous laugh and shot Jodi a sideways glance. Jodi mouthed a "whew" to her and raised her eyebrows.

"That's crazy," Kelly answered, still chuckling with nervousness. "It's a cocktail party."

"Well, anyway, most of the girls are here. A few of them should arrive any minute. Abby's coming straight from the airport. She just got in from Greece."

"Oh, wow," Kelly said.

Melissa shrugged. "She was only there for two weeks so, not much to brag about."

Kelly pursed her lips at the statement.

"Anyway, most of us are here. We're just waiting for Mother. I'll introduce you around, and then if Mother's down, maybe you can do your little demo."

"Right, sure," Kelly said with a nod.

She grasped hold of Jodi's hand and tugged her along with them. Melissa approached the group of women she'd just left.

"Hello again, ladies!" Melissa said. "Say hello to Kelly and Jodi Silverman. These are the ladies I told you about, with the pearl business."

"That's so cute that you had a pearl-themed party for Pearl," one woman said.

Melissa offered her a cat-who-caught-the-canary smile. "Thank you, MadMad!"

"Kelly, Jodi, this is Madison Montgomery." The chic brunette held out her slender hand, laden with expensive-looking rings. "Madison is one of my very best friends."

"Hey! I thought I was your very best friend," a blonde with a shoulder-length blow-out exclaimed with a giggle.

"Well, I said one of!" Melissa defended herself. "This is another of my very best friends." She laid her hand on the woman's forearm. "This is Harper Martin."

She motioned toward another woman in the group. With auburn hair, sparkling blue eyes, and a dazzling smile, the petite woman filled out her dress like a supermodel. "This is Aurora Powell, another fantastic friend. And last but certainly not least, Everly Dixon, my roommate from college."

"Hi," Kelly said, nodding her head way too much. "I'm Kelly. Nice to meet all of you."

Melissa led them across the room to a tall, slender brunette and a younger woman who resembled her. She snagged another champagne flute from a waiter on her way, taking a sip. Jodi followed her lead, grabbing two glasses and passing one off to Kelly. Kelly took a long sip of the dry beverage.

"This is my Aunt Emily and my cousin, Penelope."

"Hi, great to meet you," Emily said. She carried a cane in one hand, though she seemed to walk well enough.

"Oh, are you Pearl's sister?" Jodi inquired.

"No, actually, I'm Pearl's sister-in-law."

"Oh, okay," Kelly answered, bobbing her head again and wishing she could stop herself. "Well, I hope you both love pearls!"

"Oh, we do!" Emily said. "Penny just loves pearl jewelry."

"Of course, Penny has a *beautiful* set of heirloom pearls," Melissa responded, with a roll of her eyes. "But I'm sure she'll find a few of these pieces fun for a picnic or something."

Kelly forced her lips from a frown into a fake smile at the comment.

"Well, sorry we can't stay and chat, Auntie, but we've got to move on!"

"Nice meeting you," Emily said to Kelly, who waved as Melissa led them away.

In short order, Melissa introduced them to Reagan Walker, Pearl's cousin, and Aubrey Robinson, Reagan's daughter; Julia Palmer, Pearl's older sister, and Peyton Carter, a cousin-in-law.

Introductions were interrupted by Pearl's arrival at the party. The woman's pounding cane echoed off the walls as she smacked it against the floor with every step.

"Mother!" Melissa exclaimed. She whispered a short "excuse me" over her shoulder as she rushed to assist Pearl to a seat in the room's center. Pearl shook off her grip and rolled her eyes, before stamping over to the couch and plopping onto it.

The women gathered around her, offering their well-wishes, happy birthdays, and other schmoozing over the rich older woman. Set in a firm line, Pearl's mouth never formed a smile. She stared at most of them with narrowed eyes and an unimpressed expression.

Julia perched on the couch next to her and Peyton claimed her other side.

"Wow, must be nice to have everyone fawn all over you," Jodi said to Kelly, as they hung back from the crowd.

"She doesn't look impressed."

"She's probably used to it."

"I'm never going to remember all these names. And there's still four more people we haven't met!"

After everyone had had a chance to speak with Pearl, Melissa tapped her champagne glass. "Ladies, ladies! Yoo-hoo!"

A hushed silence fell over the room. Melissa offered another coy smile at the group. "Welcome to Willow Lake, everyone, for a *very* special occasion.

"When I first started planning mom's eightieth birthday party, all I could think of was what an incredible woman Pearl Willow is."

Jodi scrunched up her face. "Did Pearl just roll her eyes?"

Kelly studied the old woman's face. "Well, she doesn't look impressed with Melissa's speech so far, that's for sure."

"The charity work, the business connections, and of course, the fantastic daughter she raised." Melissa paused and struck a pose as a few chuckles went up through the crowd. "All of these are testaments to the caliber of woman Pearl Willow is.

"Businesswoman, philanthropist, sounding board, confidant… she's so many things to so many of us. But to me, she's Mom."

A few "awws" rose from the crowd.

"Oh, gag me," Kelly whispered to Jodi.

"She's really going for an Emmy with this speech."

"And that's why," Melissa continued, "I came up with the theme centered around the woman, the legend, Pearl. What better way to celebrate Pearl than a weekend-long Pearl party?" Melissa paused and grinned. "See what I did there?"

Another few chuckles went up through the crowd before Melissa continued.

"So, without further ado, let's get this party started!"

A cheer and applause broke out. Once they died down, Melissa continued, motioning toward Kelly and Jodi.

"Most of you have met Kelly and Jodi. For the few of you we didn't get to, there's plenty of time! We'll be spending *lots* of time together." Melissa's eyes shot skyward, and she pointed up. "As you can hear, we're socked in with rain and it's supposed to continue all weekend, so we'll be cooped up in here together all that time!"

Kelly offered a nervous laugh as she considered being trapped in this house as a storm raged day and night.

"And these two ladies will be providing us with *plenty* of fun! I asked Kelly to set up a little demo for us before dinner. So, Kelly, why don't you take it away!"

CHAPTER 5

$\mathcal{K}$elly stood frozen for a moment. All eyes rested on her. She scanned the room, an awkward smile plastered on her face. After a moment, she jumped.

"Oh! Oh, sure, right, yes. Of course. Sorry, I thought you were going for a little more of an intro there," Kelly said with a nervous chuckle, as she darted toward her table.

"Well, my name is Kelly Silverman, and this is my sister, Jodi. Ah, we're… I work with Pearls Unlimited, which is a fun and unique jewelry company."

She sank onto the chair behind the table and nervously smoothed the paper towels, before reaching for her oyster bucket. "Basically, what I do is shuck the oysters for their pearls, and then we take that pearl and set it in a jewelry piece."

Kelly's nerves settled as she continued through her familiar spiel. "Some people pick out the jewelry first, and others wait until they see the pearl's size and color before they pick their piece. We can do it either way. So, if you're not sure what you may like, we can shuck for you, and then you can let the pearl lead you!"

Kelly offered the crowd a smile. Silent faces stared back at her. She offered another nervous chuckle. "Okay, let's get started and shuck a few! I figured the first one could go to Pearl since it's her birthday!" She pulled an oyster from the bucket. It dripped its way across the table, moistening the paper towel she laid it on.

"Pearl, your first piece of jewelry is on us, as a birthday treat."

Pearl stared blankly ahead as though she couldn't care less about the show. Jodi offered her a catalog, but she waved her away. Kelly bit her lower lip and pressed on. "Okay, here we go!"

She picked up her shucking knife and slid it into the oyster. The top popped open and she pulled it back, searching the flesh for the pearl.

"Ohh! This one's lovely. I think you'll be very happy with it!" Kelly whisked it off to her salt bowl before washing it in water and wrapping it in a towel to dry it.

On her lap, Kelly set the pearl on a display board before raising it for everyone to see. "You've got a beautiful cotton candy pink!" Kelly rolled the pearl on the display board. "Nice and round with a tiny dimple here, just a little character." She lifted a shoulder as she grinned.

After showing off the pearl, she measured it. "Oh, it's nice and big! It's a seven and a half! This would be so pretty in so many of our pieces! With this color, I have a few I can recommend, or you're welcome to look through the catalog for whatever you'd like."

Kelly slid the pearl into an envelope marked with Pearl's name and scanned the crowd. "So, who's next? Anyone else want a preview opening tonight before our big party tomorrow?"

Crickets. Kelly's nose wrinkled as she attempted to keep the smile frozen on her face.

"Oh, ah, I'll take one!" Melissa called, raising her hand.

"Great!" Kelly said, as she reached into her bucket and pulled out another oyster. In short order, she had it open. Her eyes bulged as she felt around inside. "O.M.G! Melissa, you lucky girl! You've got twins!"

Kelly pulled two pearls from within the oyster and cleaned them before showing them off. "You could get a set of earrings with these; they are *very* close in color and size. These are a beautiful champagne color, both sevens."

"Oh, how fun!" Melissa said, as she sipped her champagne.

"So are you thinking of two pieces of jewelry or earrings?"

"What do you recommend?"

"Well, I *love* the 'Petal to the Metal' studs if you'd like something small. Or, if you're looking for something a little more ostentatious, the 'Heck-raising Hoops' are a nice choice."

Melissa sipped her champagne and shrugged. "Decisions, decisions. I'll have to think about it."

"Sure, take your time! I've got these set aside for you! Who's next?"

Kelly scanned the crowd but received no response.

"Well, okay, we can save all the fun for tomorrow. I know you all have lots of orders in already!"

"We probably should head in for dinner anyway," Melissa said.

Kelly set her shucking knife down and squashed the wet paper towels into a ball, stuffing them in the trash can she brought with her.

She stood and resisted the urge to smooth her skirt with her oyster juice-soaked hands. She held them up as she shuffled across the room to Melissa. "Is there a bathroom close? I'd like to wash my hands."

"Oh, sure," Melissa answered, guiding her to a powder room along the way to the dining room.

After a quick hand wash and a much-needed adjustment to her dress, she emerged, ready for the meal.

"Well, that didn't go as well as I expected," Kelly whispered to Jodi, as they continued down the hall toward the dining room.

"It'll get better," Jodi said. "They already purchased over one hundred oyster openings!"

"I'm shocked. They seem completely uninterested in the entire thing."

Jodi shrugged. "Oh well, like I said, we've already gotten hundreds of orders, so just relax and enjoy the weekend."

They entered the dining room. A long table stretched down the middle of the room. With candlelit centerpieces decorated in pearl strands, pearl-encrusted silverware, and an ornate tablecloth, the dining table looked like it came straight out of a magazine page.

Pearl sat at the head of the table. The last to arrive, Kelly and Jodi found seats at the far end of the long rectangle. Jodi took the seat on the end, and Kelly squeezed between her and an auburn-haired woman she hadn't met.

She pulled her napkin onto her lap and turned to the woman. "Hi, I'm Kelly," she said.

"Kennedy," the woman answered. "I'm a friend of the family."

"Hi, Kennedy. Nice to meet you. This is my sister, Jodi."

Kelly turned her attention to the women across the table. She hadn't met any of them yet. "Hi, I'm Kelly," she said with a wave.

"Parker Neal," the woman across the table from her said.

Her blonde hair was pulled up into a high ponytail. "I'm Pearl's niece and Melissa's cousin."

After Jodi said her hellos, the young brunette across from Kennedy introduced herself as Addison, Melissa's cousin, and Pearl's niece, explaining her mother, Pearl's sister-in-law, could not attend.

Another cousin sat across from Jodi. She glanced up from her phone long enough to say, "I'm Willow. Another niece-slash-cousin."

"Well, it's nice to meet everyone," Kelly said. "How exciting to be here for this celebration."

"Or not," Willow countered.

Kelly offered a wide-eyed smile at the others, who seemed to ignore the young woman's bad attitude.

"This house is so unique," Jodi said. "We found a room with a carousel in it!"

"Whoop-de-do," Willow grumbled, twirling a finger in the air.

"Like you didn't enjoy it when you were a kid, Willow," Addison shot back.

"Whenever Aunt Pearl allowed us to grace her with our presence."

"She wasn't that bad to you," Parker said.

"Let's not get into it," Willow snapped.

"What did you come for?" Addison questioned.

"Like we had a choice," Willow answered. "Melissa would have blown her top if we didn't show."

"And when have you ever cared about that?" Parker questioned, as Melissa stood from a chair positioned near the center of the table's length.

She tapped her glass to garner everyone's attention. A hushed silence fell over the room. Melissa waited until she had all eyes on her. She scanned the faces around the table, a coy smile on her face.

"Welcome, again, everyone," she began, "to what I hope will be a wonderful weekend-long celebration of a remarkable woman, my mother, Pearl."

Jodi leaned toward Kelly and whispered, "Didn't she do the speech thing already?"

"She'll do it ten more times before the weekend is out," Willow said. "She loves the limelight."

Melissa continued, waving her glass around in the air. "Before we start with the first course, I'd like to offer a few words about my mother."

"Oh, Melissa, just sit down," Pearl roared.

Melissa fluttered her eyelashes at her mother's comment. "Oh, Mother," she said, glancing around with an awkward smile. "Always so reluctant to accept praise. I just wanted to say a few words then let everyone else chime in."

Pearl rolled her eyes. "You wanted the attention on you like you always do. And the rest of you, don't think I don't know why you're here. You want my money. You want to keep your spot in the will. Bunch of money grubbers is all you are."

Kelly's eyes went wide as she listened to the scathing speech. "Whoa," she whispered to Jodi.

Pearl continued on her rant, "You can't stand each other, but you're lined up to be at every event so you can appear in my will. Don't think I don't know what you're all up to. Well, I got news for you. I'm not planning on dying anytime soon. So you've got a long wait on your hands."

"Mother," Melissa tried, her jaw tightening, displaying her clear annoyance with the situation.

"Sit down, Melissa, and shut up. Let's just get this weekend over with." Pearl twisted to glance over her shoulder at a man dressed in a butler's uniform. She snapped her fingers and shouted, "Roberto! Let's eat."

With a sour expression and shake of her head, Pearl

whisked her napkin onto her lap. Melissa sank into her seat and sipped at her champagne. She winced as she turned toward Aurora, seated to her right, and whispered something, shaking her head.

Thunder boomed overhead and the lights flickered as the serving staff burst from the double doors across the room.

"I hope the food's good," Jodi mumbled.

Dishes clattered as the first course, a cold mango soup, was served, and everyone dug in. Conversation resumed around the table as the shock of Pearl's outburst wore off. Kelly flicked her gaze to an open seat across from Melissa. The empty chair must have been for Abby, who she recalled was coming from the airport. She wondered if she'd make it given the weather. The storm seemed to rage on, pummeling the house with rain and hail and generating a tremendous amount of thunder and lightning.

As the serving staff cleared away the first course, the lights flickered again. "I really hope the power doesn't go out," Kelly said.

As if on cue, the lights dimmed again and then went dark. Kelly reached out to clutch Jodi's hand. A few gasps sounded in the darkened room. In a moment, they popped back on.

A new woman stood in the doorway. In a sleek pantsuit and wide-brimmed hat, she struck a pose.

"Well, talk about making an entrance!" she exclaimed to the hushed diners.

A few chuckles emerged from the crowd, and Melissa leapt from her seat and raced over to the woman and embraced her. "Abby! You made it!"

"And not a moment too soon!" the woman announced, as they strode arm-in-arm to the table. "I hope none of you are planning on leaving. The roads are *gone*."

"What?" Emily questioned.

"Literally, the road washed out behind us as the driver

drove me here. He's stuck here, too. I'll probably have to pay him for the weekend." Abby rolled her eyes at the statement and waved her hands in the air. "Ugh, never mind my troubles though. We're here for a party, right?"

"Well, she's certainly lively," Kelly said.

"Are the roads really washed out, do you think, or is she just being dramatic?" Jodi asked.

"We're probably stuck here," Willow said. "Happens all the time in weather like this."

Addison nodded, adding, "The little bridge just before you climb up to the house is probably submerged."

"And it's supposed to keep raining through tomorrow night. We'll be lucky to be leaving by Sunday."

Kelly winced as she considered being stuck in the creepiest house she'd ever stayed in. She swallowed hard, letting her eyes float around the room, taking in all the gothic architecture.

"At least we're stuck somewhere nice!" Jodi exclaimed next to her.

Kelly struggled to not roll her eyes at the statement.

The rest of the meal continued without any additional surprises and no further blackouts. The storm continued to pummel the area, giving Kelly a start a few times. As they finished their dessert, a baked Alaska, the lights flickered again.

"Is there a generator in this house?" Kelly inquired.

"Yes," Parker answered. "Don't worry, if the lights go out, they won't be off for long."

Kelly smiled and nodded, pleased with the answer. As she swallowed her last bite, Melissa rose.

"Another speech?" Jodi questioned.

"Ladies! If you'd all like to join me in the sitting room for post-dinner drinks, we'll be showing a slideshow of Pearl's life."

Chatter resumed as the ladies began to leave their seats and make their way down the wide hall and across the foyer to the sitting room. A large screen had been set up across from the sofa.

Pearl wandered in and plopped in the center of the couch. The waitstaff filtered through with more champagne. Kelly and Jodi snagged another glass.

"We might need this," Kelly said, as she eyed the screen.

"Yeah," Jodi agreed. "I hope Pearl doesn't have another outburst like she did at dinner. Talk about uncomfortable."

Kelly nodded, her eyebrows shooting high as she sipped at the pink champagne. The lights flickered again before reviving. Melissa fiddled with a remote, waving it at the screen until a blue light shone on it. After a moment, and a bit more fiddling on Melissa's part, an image sprang to life. With one more emphatic push on the remote, music filled the air, and pictures of Pearl as a baby floated across the screen, captions appearing below them.

"Even as a baby, Pearl was incredible!" the screen boasted.

"Wow, it's getting deep," Kelly murmured.

"No kidding," Jodi said.

Thunder boomed overhead again, and lightning flashed through the windows. The video played for another minute, before another massive clap of thunder shook the house. The loud bang made everyone jump. Then the room plunged into darkness.

Women shouted as the lights went out and the music slowed to a stop. Kelly reached blindly to her left and clamped her hand onto Jodi's arm. At least, she hoped it was Jodi's arm.

"Great!" she groaned. Movement swept around the room. Someone bumped into Kelly, sending her spiraling forward as she desperately attempted to keep her balance. A croaking groan sounded, before everything whirred back to life.

Jodi grasped Kelly to prevent her from falling. "Whew, thanks," she said, as the lights came up. The music resumed and pictures continued to parade across the now-lit screen.

"That was scary," Kelly murmured, glancing at Jodi. Jodi's jaw hung open and her face was two shades paler than normal. "What's wrong with you?"

Jodi's lower lip bobbed up and down, but no noise emerged. A look of panicked terror wrinkled her forehead.

Without a word, Jodi pointed toward the sofa. Gasps began to ring out from the group. Kelly followed the line of Jodi's pointed finger, her eyes widening as she spotted the scene.

"Oh my goodness!" she exclaimed, her hand shooting up to cover her gaping mouth.

Across the room, sprawled on the sofa sat Pearl. With her eyes closed and her limbs slack, Kelly's shucking knife stuck out from Pearl's chest.

Gasps rang out across the room as the lights glowed to life. The sound of smashing glass hit Kelly's ears as Pearl's sister, Julia, dropped her champagne glass. Her hands clutched at her cheeks as she shrieked, before her eyes rolled back in her head and she slipped to the floor.

Kelly sprinted across the room, nearly twisting an ankle in her heels, and scooped the woman up before she hit the hardwood. Her champagne sloshed in the glass still clutched in her hand, threatening to spill over onto the area rug.

Reagan and her daughter, Aubrey, hurried across the room, aiding Kelly in easing the faint woman to an armchair.

"Someone call 9-1-1!" one of the women shouted, though Kelly couldn't say which of them.

Across the room, Jodi already had her phone pressed to her ear. Melissa's friends gathered around her as she slumped on weak legs, her eyes rolling back. With pinched faces, they hovered over the woman. Aurora fanned her with one of Kelly's catalogs while Everly rubbed her arm, and another woman, whose name Kelly had already forgotten, stroked her hair.

Confusion reigned as some women attempted to tend to the deceased, while others raced from the room. A few women milled around, biting their fingernails, or rubbing their necks in agitation.

After a few moments passed, Penelope shook her head.

"She's dead," she announced, as the bright red stain on Pearl's light pink dress bloomed into a larger circle. Her mother, Emily, sitting on Pearl's other side, bit her lower lip as she clutched Pearl's lifeless hand. A tear rolled down her cheek.

Jodi murmured a few words into the phone, reporting to the 9-1-1 operator that Pearl was deceased. After a few moments, she ended the call. The butler hurried into the room, his face white, as one of the women unfurled a blanket and placed it over Pearl's dead form. The knife stuck out, pushing the blanket into a grotesque shape as a constant reminder of what lay beneath.

"The police are on their way, but when I told them the location," Jodi announced, "they weren't sure they could make it."

"What did they say to do?" Abby questioned.

"Sit tight and don't touch anything," Jodi answered.

"Sit tight?" Peyton exclaimed. "Are you kidding?"

"Pearl's dead!" Parker shouted. "And the police say to sit tight?"

Julia moaned and thrashed her head as she came to in the armchair. She stared at the sheet over Pearl before bursting into tears. Sobs wracked the woman's shoulders, and she buried her face in her hands.

"I'm not sitting tight," Addison said, storming across the room. "I'm leaving!"

"Ha!" Willow said, a chuckle escaping her lips. "Where are you going to go? The roads are washed out. You can't leave."

Jodi's phone rang. She swiped to answer it, murmuring a few words before she nodded and hung up.

"Folks!" she shouted over the din of the room. "That was the police. The bridge leading here is gone. They are working to get someone up to the house, but it's not going to happen tonight."

Everyone in the room stood in stunned silence. "Well, what are we supposed to do?" one of the women shouted.

"Are we supposed to just leave Pearl here?"

"We can't leave her there with a knife stuck in her chest!"

Julia resumed her wailing at the words.

"Might I suggest, Miss Melissa, that we place her in the walk-in freezer?" the butler said, his hands clutched behind his back.

Melissa swooned again at the words. No one else made a move to do anything.

"Okay, I think that's probably a good idea," Kelly said. "Just keep everything intact and move her."

"Oh, I'm so glad the hired help thinks so," Madison retorted.

"Hey!" Kelly answered.

"Someone has to do something," Jodi said in Kelly's defense.

"Of course you want to move the body," Harper shouted. "You probably killed her. Best way to ruin a crime scene is to destroy it."

Kelly screwed up her face. "What? Why would I kill her? I just met her!"

"It's your knife in her chest!" Harper accused.

"Yes!" Kelly answered. "My shucking knife, that was out on the table for anyone to grab!" She swung her arm to the table, gesturing emphatically.

Harper rolled her eyes. "Why would any of *us* kill Pearl?" She crossed her arms tightly over her chest.

Kelly crinkled her forehead as she searched for words.

"Well, someone did," Jodi said.

"And it wasn't me," Kelly added.

"She's right," Willow answered. "One of us is a murderer. And it looks like we're stuck here *all* weekend long. I wonder how many more bodies will drop before Sunday hits."

"Stop being so boorish, Willow," Parker snapped.

"It's the truth," Willow retorted, raising her eyebrows and cocking her head.

"Look, I think we need to move Pearl's body, and everyone needs to go to their neutral corners. Hopefully, the police will get here soon and sort this all out," Kelly said.

"Until then, I guess we just have to deal with the fact that someone here committed a horrible crime," Harper huffed.

Kelly refrained from answering as the butler retrieved two servers to move Pearl from her spot on the sofa. As the two men lifted her, Pearl's arm slid from its resting spot on the couch, dangling for a moment before making a sickening smack against the coffee table.

Screams emerged from several women. Kelly winced, her stomach turning over as they tossed her arm onto her chest before hauling her limp form from the room.

The women milled around for a few moments before Aurora and Everly escorted Melissa from the room to lay down. Reagan also suggested Julia return to her bedroom.

"Guess we should head up," Kelly said to Jodi.

Jodi agreed with a nod and the two women started across the room.

"Wait a minute!" someone shouted behind them. "Where are you going?"

Kelly spun to face the others. "Up to our rooms."

"I don't think so," Harper said. "You've got some explaining to do."

"Excuse me?" Kelly answered.

"It's *your* knife in her chest."

Kelly's jaw dropped open. "I didn't kill her!" she exclaimed.

"Then who did?" Harper asked, scanning the room. "No one's leaving this room until someone confesses. Someone just killed my best friend's mother, and I'm going to find out who. For Melissa."

Willow rolled her eyes as she stalked across the room. "Good luck with that!"

"Get back here!" Harper shouted.

Willow waved over her head as she continued through the doors and into the foyer.

"No one made you boss, Harper," Madison said. "We all want to help Melissa, but being a self-proclaimed detective is a little much."

"I'm with Willow," Addison replied, crossing the room. "I'll be in my room."

The women slowly started to filter from the space, leaving an annoyed Harper behind.

Kelly and Jodi slogged through the halls to their rooms. Kelly pulled her heels off as she ambled through the door and collapsed on Jodi's bed. Throwing herself backward onto the soft duvet, she sighed.

"I can't believe this."

"Really," Jodi murmured. "Talk about a killer party."

"Literally," Kelly agreed.

Jodi sank onto the bed and pulled off her shoes before sliding off her bangles.

After a few moments, Kelly rolled over and stared at her sister. She propped her head up on her hand, resting her elbow on the cushy mattress.

"Who do you think did it?"

Jodi shrugged as she unclasped her necklace. "I'm not sure."

Kelly's brow furrowed and she grabbed the necklace around her neck, sliding the pendant back and forth on the chain as she pondered their situation. "Someone did it," she murmured.

"Yeah, that's obvious," Jodi answered, bouncing off the bed and to the floor. She padded across the parquet and dug around in her suitcase, before pulling out a robe and pajamas.

She tossed them on the bed next to Kelly and then unzipped her dress. With a sigh, Jodi said, "I can't believe someone was just murdered."

"It's really hitting home now that the commotion is over," Kelly agreed. "Oh, those look so comfortable." She eyed Jodi's soft pink pajamas.

"Go change," Jodi answered.

Kelly winced and shivered. "I don't want to be alone."

Jodi shot her a questioning glance.

"Someone just died! In a creepy house. And it's storming out."

"Just grab your stuff and come back in here."

"Okay," Kelly said. She slid to the floor and hurried across the room and through the shared bathroom. A loud clap of thunder peeled through the silence as she entered her room. Kelly winced and sprinted to her suitcase, digging through frantically for her pajamas and robe. With the items in hand, she ran back to Jodi's room.

"Oh, you made it. You're still alive!" Jodi said, sarcasm dripping from her voice.

"Haha, Jodi," Kelly replied, as she stripped off the dress and tossed it at her sister. "Here's your dress back. I think it's more than understandable that I'm a little nervous. Someone was just killed, and the murderer is still walking around free! She could strike again!" She tugged her pajama top over her head.

"Why would she kill us, though? Killing Pearl seemed personal."

"Oh, I don't know. She used *my* knife to do it, so maybe she'll kill me next," Kelly said, as she slid on her pajama bottoms.

"That's a stretch."

"Oh, right. About as much of a stretch as whatever-her-name-is accusing me of killing Pearl. And she was pretty adamant."

"Harper. It's Harper who accused you."

"Oh, right," Kelly said, flinging her arms out before she wrapped her robe around her and tossed herself onto Jodi's bed. "How could I forget that! Maybe it's because almost everyone here has a ridiculous name. Who names their child Harper?"

"Same people who name their child Everly," Jodi retorted with a snort.

"Or Addison."

"Parker."

"Peyton."

"Well, Peyton Manning," Jodi pointed out.

"Who is a man, not a woman, and still, it's just as ridiculous for a man."

Silence fell between them as they pondered the naming conventions of the Barlow family and friends.

Kelly heaved a sigh. "We should have brought snacks."

"Maybe we could raid the kitchen."

"Oh, yeah, great," Kelly said. "Maybe we'll run into the murderer, and they'll kill us, too!"

"We could take a weapon. Did you bring an extra shucking knife?"

"Yeah, I did," Kelly noted. "But I'm not sure creeping around in this place with a knife in my hands is going to make me look any less guilty."

"No one actually thinks you did it except Harper."

"Well, and the killer, who would *love* to pin this on me." Kelly's eyebrows shot up. "OMG, do you think Harper is the killer?"

"Why would Harper be the killer?"

"I don't know," Kelly said, her shoulders sagging. "I just want to know who it is, so they stop accusing me. And so we can avoid them, so they don't kill us." Kelly's gaze found the door across the room. "Maybe we should lock our doors."

Jodi climbed off the bed and slid into her slippers. She padded across the room and grabbed the door handle.

"Where are you going?"

"Didn't you want a snack?"

"Jodi!" Kelly said, bolting upright. "You can't go wandering around with a murderer on the loose!"

"Then you'd better come with me."

"Wait," Kelly said, hurrying off the bed. "I'll get my knife."

"Hurry up!" Jodi called as Kelly hastened through the shared bathroom, robe flying behind her. She pawed through her pearl party paraphernalia in search of her second knife. As she sorted through the duffel bag in search of the item, likely buried at the bottom, a shuffling sound reached her ears.

Assuming it was Jodi, she called, "Yeah, I'm trying!"

"Huh?" she heard Jodi call from the other room.

Kelly swiveled her head to glance over her shoulder. Jodi was nowhere in sight. The shuffling sounded again, and Kelly snapped her head in the opposite direction, narrowing her eyes at the door leading to the hallway.

The sound came from outside the door. Kelly dropped the materials in her bag and raced across the room, flicking the lights off. Light shined under the door. A shadow darkened a spot outside her room.

CHAPTER 7

Kelly's eyes went wide. Someone was hovering outside her door. She flicked the lights on and sprinted across the room. Her fingers fumbled to turn the lock. She backed away, plastering the hair behind her ears as she stared at the wooden barrier. The lion's head doorknob slowly began to twist as someone tried to gain entry to the room.

Kelly's eyes bulged as she bumped into a small table in the room. It screeched across the floor, causing her to wince. The knob ceased moving. Kelly pursed her lips, holding her breath as she waited to determine if the person on the opposite side of the door would leave or not. She sidestepped her way back to her pearl party duffel bag and frantically dug through it in search of her knife. She discovered it in its protective case at the bottom of the bag.

Yanking it free, Kelly tightened her grip on the knife's hilt and returned her attention to the door. The knob began to twist back and forth quickly. Kelly squeezed her lips together and raised the knife above her head.

Thoughts crowded into her mind. Who was on the opposite side of the door? Was it the killer? Would the lock hold? If it didn't, could she actually use her knife to protect herself? Would she freeze? Would she end up murdered?

The door handle stopped moving again. Kelly bit her lower lip as she backed toward the bathroom. She inched through the doorway and slammed the door shut, locking it too. She hurried across the space and into Jodi's room.

"Took you long enough," Jodi said from the armchair.

"Someone's out there!"

"Huh?"

"Someone's out there!" Kelly repeated in a whispered tone, her voice choppy from gasping for panicked breaths.

Jodi furrowed her brow and stalked back to the door. "No!" Kelly shouted. "Don't open it! It could be the killer."

Jodi rolled her eyes and tugged the door open. She glanced into the hallway, her head swiveling left and right. "There's no one here."

"What?" Kelly questioned, dropping the knife to her side. She stormed across the room and yanked open the second door. She searched the hall outside. Empty.

"Wh – but –" she spit out, as she swiveled to check the other side of the hall. "Someone was there. They were turning that stupid creepy lion's head doorknob."

Jodi's eyebrows shot up to her hairline.

"I'm serious!" Kelly said. "I could see their shadow. Then they started messing with the doorknob."

"Why didn't they just open it?"

"Because I locked the door."

"Wait, wait," Jodi answered, holding her hand up in the air. "When did you lock the door?"

"After I saw the person outside."

Jodi rolled her eyes.

"What?" Kelly questioned.

"They waited for you to lock the door before they tried to come in?"

Kelly lifted a shoulder as she screwed up her face. "I guess so."

"Ooooookay," Jodi mumbled. "Come on, let's go get that snack." Jodi began down the hall.

"Jodi!" Kelly exclaimed, hurrying after her. "Someone was at my door!"

"I think you're seeing things. Why would someone try to get in after you locked the door?"

"Maybe they were listening at the door and then tried it after I locked it."

"It's a stretch."

"It's no more of a stretch than–"

"–than Harper calling you a murderer, I know, I know."

"Do you think it was Harper?"

Jodi shrugged as they approached the massive stairs leading to the foyer. "Ugh," Kelly groaned, "these steps again."

They plodded down the forty or so odd stairs. "I'm going to lose ten pounds before we leave here."

"Well, that's something to look forward to, right?"

"Yes, I'll be ten pounds lighter in my casket after we're murdered in our sleep. Where's the kitchen?" Kelly asked, her head swiveling around the foyer.

"I was going to go to the dining room, then through those doors the servers came through to find it."

"Oh, good thinking, Jodi," Kelly said, as they started down the hall.

"You don't think they keep the ice cream in the walk-in freezer, do you?"

"I don't know. Why? Oooooh," Kelly murmured, as realization dawned on her.

"Yeah, I'd rather not see the body again."

"Me either," Kelly said, with a scrunched-up nose.

They pushed through the doors into the dining room and crossed the space to a door. Jodi pushed it open and stared inside. "Stairs," she reported.

"Oh, great. Leading to a dungeon where they've stored the body."

"Price we'll have to pay for ice cream."

"We should try to find something else, too. Like pretzels or something."

"Pretzels and ice cream?" Jodi questioned, as they descended the stairs.

"No, ice cream for now. Pretzels for later."

Jodi shot her a look.

"I don't want to come back down here to body central again."

"Okay," Jodi agreed as they entered the enormous kitchen. "Wow, this is huge!"

"It looks like the kitchen from a restaurant," Kelly said, as she swiped her hand over the granite island countertop with rich, dark cabinets below. Ovens lined one piece of the wall from top to bottom. A large stainless-steel side-by-side refrigerator stood on the far wall. A stainless-steel door with a thick hinge stood next to it.

"That must be the walk-in freezer," Kelly whispered.

"Yeah."

Kelly stared at it. "Should we open it?"

"Why?" Jodi asked, incredulous.

"To see if her body is still there."

"Where else would it be? And why are you whispering?"

"Oh, I don't know," she said, her voice returning to normal. "Maybe the body is roaming around the halls. I wouldn't be shocked in a house like this."

Kelly crossed to the door, her fingers lingering on the handle.

"Don't open it!" Jodi warned.

"Why not?!"

Jodi shrugged. Kelly pulled the handle, releasing the seal on the door. She tugged the door open. Cold air rushed out. On the floor, a sheet cloaked a lumpy form. The characteristic hilt of the knife stuck up from the figure's chest.

"Happy now?" Jodi inquired.

"Very," Kelly said. "She's still there and so is the knife."

"Now, let's get the snacks and get out of here."

Kelly tiptoed over to the refrigerator. "I hope the ice cream's in this freezer."

Jodi searched through the cupboards. Kelly spotted an open door to her left. "Jodi! Pantry."

"There's got to be snacks in there!" Jodi answered, making her way across the kitchen toward it.

Kelly tugged open the heavy freezer door of the massive fridge. A puff of frosty air greeted her. She studied the inside, moving various things around in search of ice cream. A large five-gallon tub of chocolate ice cream hid behind a stack of frozen dinners.

Kelly shoved them aside and pulled the tub out by its red handle.

"Really?" Jodi asked as Kelly closed the door. Kelly spun, her eyes wide, before biting her lower lip, the huge tub of ice cream clutched in her hand.

Kelly gave a quick shake to her head. "No, I was going to just find a few bowls."

After scouring the cupboards, they found bowls, spoons, and an ice cream scoop. With ice cream brimming over the edges of their bowls, one bag of pretzels, and another of cheese popcorn, they headed for their room. Kelly stuffed her knife into her robe pocket, keeping her hands free to carry their loot.

They climbed the stairs and skirted through the dining room and down the hall toward the foyer.

"This ice cream is going to be totally worth it after these stairs," Kelly groaned, as they climbed the last few to the second floor.

"Good thing we brought the extra snacks," Jodi agreed.

They wound through the halls, seeking their bedrooms. After the second left, hushed voices floated down the hall from around a corner.

Kelly stopped walking, her eyes going wide. She crept toward the other hall. With her head, she silently motioned for Jodi to inch closer. She pursed her lips and raised her eyebrows, as she pulsed her head in the air toward the sound of the voices.

"… can't believe she did this!"

"We don't know that!"

"Oh, come on, who else did?"

Kelly raised her eyebrows at Jodi. "Who is it?" she mouthed.

Jodi shrugged and shook her head. As she moved, the popcorn bag crinkled. Kelly winced and held her hand up to signal Jodi to stay still.

Jodi frowned at her in response.

The quiet conversation continued down the hall after a brief pause. "Just don't jump to conclusions."

"It couldn't be anyone else. She's wanted the old lady gone for years. I can't believe she actually did it."

"I'm not convinced."

"Oh, come off of it, Maddie. We both know Melissa killed her mother!"

CHAPTER 8

Kelly's jaw unhinged at the statement, and she stiffened. Her sudden movement caused the spoon, precariously teetering on a mound of ice cream, to topple from the bowl. It clattered to the floor, bouncing around on the hardwood floor before rattling to a stop.

"Hello?!" a voice called down the hall.

"*Shoot!*" Kelly hissed. She snatched the spoon from the floor, dropping the bag of pretzels. "Crap!"

"Is someone there?"

She snagged the bag's corner with two fingers as she palmed the spoon. "Run!" she breathed to Jodi.

They hurried down the hall, taking the first turn they found, winding through halls they'd never seen before.

Kelly stopped three halls away, leaning against the wall and gulping in air. "Who was that?"

Jodi shrugged, her chest heaving as she rested against the opposite wall. "Don't know. But she said Maddie. So one of them was Maddie."

"And they think Melissa did it!"

"I can't believe that."

"Neither could Maddie," Kelly answered. "Who was the other woman? The one who thinks Melissa did it?"

"We might have found out if you hadn't dropped your spoon like a big klutz."

"Sorry!" Kelly said.

"You *had* to have that last scoop."

"I said I'm sorry!" Kelly exclaimed, readjusting the pretzel bag under her arm as she glanced around. "Where are we, anyway?"

"No idea. I got lost three halls ago."

"We need to find our way to our rooms. We can't go back that way, though."

"Why not?"

"What if they're still there?"

"We act like we just came up from the kitchen and have no idea who that other person could have been."

"Except I'm carrying the offending spoon!" Kelly exclaimed, waving the spoon in the air.

"Fine, we'll keep wandering until the ice cream melts."

"Well, good," Kelly said, continuing down the hall, "because I like melted ice cream."

They meandered down the wide ornate hall, their slippers padding over the thick red carpet that painted a stripe down the middle of the hall.

"It's got to be back this way," Kelly said, hanging a left.

They reached a curved stairway leading up. "This isn't right," Jodi replied.

"No kidding," Kelly answered, retracing her steps, and heading right at the fork in the halls.

She turned right again, finding a set of double doors at the end of a hallway. "Nope," Kelly said with a sigh.

"We're going to have to go back the way we came!" Jodi insisted.

"No! I'm not getting us caught!"

"Okay, we'll keep wandering through halls that *won't* lead us to our bedroom, so we don't get caught."

"Okay, okay, fine."

They retraced their steps to the best of their ability, finding the hall that contained the whispering ladies earlier.

Kelly peered around the corner before they entered the hall. "Coast's clear," she whispered.

Kelly sidestepped to the hall's entrance. She stared down the length of it, biting her lower lip. After a moment, she raised her chin and rolled her shoulders back.

"Let's go," she said, with a nod.

They sauntered down the hall. As they reached the halfway point, Kelly quickened her pace. "Slow down!" Jodi exclaimed.

"Just–" Kelly began, when a door swung open.

Kelly winced and swung in a circle, hurrying back down the hall.

"Kelly? Jodi?" Madison called after them.

Kelly scrunched her lips together and squeezed her eyes closed. She plastered a smile onto her face and spun on her heel, facing the brunette. Her smile faltered as she faced her. Madison stepped out into the hall, an ankle-length silk robe fluttering around her, doing little to cover the silk nighty that barely covered her perfectly tanned thighs. High-heeled slippers with feather puffs completed her ensemble.

Holding back an eye roll, she widened her grin again. "Maddie, hi!" she exclaimed, her voice two octaves higher than normal.

Madison gave her a half-chuckle, half-huff, wiggling her eyebrows. "I prefer Madison," she said. "Were you ladies here a few moments ago?"

"Us?" Kelly questioned, eyes wide with surprise. She glanced at Jodi before forcing a laugh. "No! Obviously, we were downstairs getting ice cream!"

Madison eyed their bowls and the bags tucked under each arm. "And then some," she noted.

"Why? Did you hear something? Or see something?" Kelly asked. Madison didn't answer for a moment, so Kelly continued to babble nervously. "Cause I could have sworn that I heard someone at my door like right before we went down for the ice cream."

"No, nothing like that," Madison said. "Everly and I were talking and thought we heard someone in the hall listening to our conversation."

Kelly feigned shock. "Oh! Wow! Well, I don't know who that could have been because we were downstairs getting ice cream. So…"

Madison crossed her arms over her chest and eyed them, her lips puckered. "Funny, because I could have sworn I heard the sound of a spoon hitting the floor."

Kelly lifted her shoulders toward her ears. "So weird. Maybe someone else had a craving for ice cream, too."

Madison stared at them for another moment before Kelly excused them. "Well, we'd better get back to our rooms before this melts!" She waved her bowl in the air. "Have a good night!"

Kelly hurried down the hall past the woman with Jodi trailing behind her. She jetted around the corner and blew out a breath in relief.

"Wow, that couldn't have been any more awkward," she said to Jodi, as they finally rounded the corner into their hallway.

"Well, if you weren't babbling like you were guilty as sin," Jodi said.

"I couldn't help it! I was so nervous!"

"Why? We didn't do anything wrong."

"Jodi!" Kelly exclaimed, as she wrangled the door handle

with the hand clutching her spoon. "One of these people is a killer! And we have no idea who! We can't be too careful."

"Okay, okay, point taken. But Everly, who we now know was the other woman in the hall, thinks it was Melissa."

Jodi kicked the door shut with her foot. Kelly hurried across the room and dumped the bag of pretzels on the bed, sliding her ice cream bowl onto the night table. She darted back to the door and locked it.

"Do you really think Melissa killed her own mother?" Kelly asked, as she climbed onto the bed next to Jodi and grabbed her ice cream bowl.

Jodi considered it as she slid the spoon from her mouth. "Mmm, this ice cream seems better than the kind we get."

"Jodi!" Kelly shouted. "Do you really think Melissa killed her mother?"

Jodi puckered her lips and stared at her bowl. "I wonder how much they pay for this. I bet it's more than we pay at the grocery store."

Kelly huffed and pushed the half-melted ice cream around in her bowl. Jodi side-eyed her. With a roll of her eyes, she said, "I don't know if Melissa killed her. How would I know?"

"Make an educated guess."

Jodi raised her shoulders to her ears. Her lips bobbed up and down, but no words came out. After a few moments, she said, "No? I don't know. I'm not sure."

"Okay, your initial reaction was no, so I'm going to go with that as your gut reaction. We both know I didn't kill Pearl, and Melissa probably didn't kill her own mother. So who did?"

"We barely know any of these people. We can't solve this, Kelly. We should just let the police handle it when they get here."

"I'd feel more comfortable if we had a direction to point

them in. Any evidence is likely compromised now. And everyone's memories will be hazy by the time they arrive, even if it's tomorrow."

"So? It's their problem."

"It's *our* problem if Harper runs her mouth about me being the culprit."

"No one's going to believe that."

"Oh really? Really?" Kelly inquired, bouncing around on the bed to face Jodi. "Will the police just take my word for it? Or will I get hauled downtown and harassed while they sort this out? Plus, my prints are all over that knife."

Jodi sighed. "I guess you have a point, but I don't think we stand a good chance of solving this."

"You never know until you try." Kelly scooped up the last spoonful of ice cream, licked the spoon clean, and tossed it into her bowl. It clattered around the ceramic as she shoved the bowl onto the night table and leapt from the bed. "Be right back."

She tiptoed across the room in bare feet and disappeared through the bathroom door. With her laptop and a notebook and pen in hand, she returned. "You'd think they'd spring for heated floors in this place."

She tossed her stuff onto the bed and climbed on top. "Okay, first we need to make a list of everyone. Then we need to write any motives they might have or reasons they couldn't have killed Pearl." She tapped her laptop. "I brought this in case we can't remember someone's name. If they placed an order, we've got their name."

"Okay, number one. Melissa," Jodi said.

Kelly nodded and jotted her name on the pad. "Melissa Barlow. Motive, what?" she said, tapping the pen against her lips.

"Money," Jodi said.

Kelly nodded as she wrote it next to Melissa's name.

Jodi continued, "Presumably, Pearl has all the money and Melissa will get all of it when she dies."

"Right. Excellent motivation to kill her. Any others?"

"Uh…" Jodi murmured.

"Oh!" Kelly exclaimed. "Her mother was really mean to her."

Jodi wrinkled her brow and snapped her eyes to Kelly. "Seriously?"

"Well, she was! We both heard that nasty speech."

"Still, your mom is mean to you, so you off her?"

"It could happen."

"Okay, fine," Jodi said. "Write it down."

Kelly nodded and slid the pen across the paper to jot the note. "Okay," she answered, as she emphatically jabbed the pen against the paper to place a period. "Anything else?"

"Mmmm, can't think of anything."

"Okay, reasons she couldn't have killed her?"

"She was her mother," Jodi said.

Kelly's eyes searched the room as she considered it. "But is that really a reason *not* to kill someone?"

"Yes?" Jodi replied, her tone questioning.

"I was thinking more like she wasn't in the room or something."

"But she was."

"But you know what I mean," Kelly said. "Like she wasn't near the knife, or she was too far away to have made it in time. That kind of thing."

"Ohhh – opportunity."

"Yes," Kelly said with a nod, pointing the pen at her. "Motive, means, and opportunity. So, the way I see it, everyone had means, but not everyone had motive and opportunity."

Jodi scrunched up her face. "Or did everyone have opportunity, but not the motive and means?"

Kelly frowned. "Well, not everyone has motive, right?"

"We don't know that, but I get where you're going."

"So, how is opportunity different than means?"

"Means is… I don't know," Jodi answered.

"Means is when you have the means to do it."

"You can't use the word in the definition, Kelly."

"Well, I mean, how else can we say it? Means is when you can do it."

"Or is that opportunity? Like you have the opportunity, so that's when you can do it?"

"I don't know," Kelly replied, after a moment.

"Look it up."

"Right," Kelly said, setting the notebook down before dragging her laptop onto her legs.

She pulled open the top and tapped around. After a moment, she dropped her head between her shoulders with a sigh. "No Wi-Fi."

"What? Ohhhh," Jodi said. "You need the password."

"Yep," Kelly responded with a nod. "How could I forget to ask Melissa? Probably because I was so busy dragging all the luggage in with no help while you and Melissa ran off ahead of me."

"Oh, sure, blame me."

"Well, I can't go ask her now. I'll have to use my phone." Kelly shoved the laptop to the side and climbed off the bed, heading for her room.

She made it halfway across when Jodi threw her arms in the air. "Wait!" she shouted.

"What is it?" Kelly asked, freezing in place, fingers spread and a terrified look on her face. "Is someone at the door?"

"No," Jodi said, leaping off the bed and running toward her purse. "Oh, wow, this floor is cold."

"Jodi!"

Jodi rummaged through her purse and pulled out a folded

note. "Melissa gave me the Wi-Fi password earlier! She said in case we needed it for the orders."

Kelly's shoulders slumped and she rolled her eyes. "You couldn't have remembered that before?"

"Sorry! I was busy examining motive and means."

"Or opportunity, we haven't figured out which yet."

They both climbed onto the bed and Kelly opened her laptop again. She swiped the paper from Jodi and input the password. "There! We're in! Okay, means and opportunity."

Kelly's fingers clattered across the keyboard as she typed. "Okay, here. Means is the ability and tools necessary to commit the crime. Opportunity is the adequate chance to commit the crime."

Jodi nodded. After a moment, she said, "So, what does that mean?"

"Well," Kelly said, pausing before she continued, "Means would be the ability and tools, so let's see, everyone had access to the tool, which was the knife."

"And everyone seemed capable of stabbing her, right?"

Kelly nodded. "Right, no one is physically challenged or anything like that, so everyone had means."

"Okay, opportunity, then," Jodi said.

"Not everyone had opportunity, right?"

"Well, they did," Jodi answered. "They were all in the room."

"Are we sure?"

Jodi pursed her lips in thought. "I think so."

"Do you think, or do you know?"

"I think," Jodi repeated, as she flicked her gaze to Kelly for a moment. She returned her eyes forward and pursed her lips as she continued to think.

"Okay, wait, let's make a list of everyone here and go from there. We'll note whether they were in the room, not in the room or we're not certain."

"Okay."

"So we have Melissa. She was definitely there."

"Yep," Jodi confirmed. "Because she fainted when she saw her mother."

"Right," Kelly said, waving her pen in the air. She jotted the note down on her sheet. "Who was with her when she fainted? Two people helped her, right?"

"Uhhh," Jodi murmured. "There was a whole group of them."

"And I never know their names."

"Write all the names down first."

"Okay, okay." Kelly waved her hands in the air. "Abby. The one coming from Greece."

"Right," Jodi said. "But she only went to Greece for a few weeks."

"The loser," Kelly added.

"Yeah, what a waste to go for that short of a time."

"It's definitely nothing to brag about." The sisters chuckled over the ridiculous conversation. "Okay, was Abby in the room?"

Jodi closed her eyes and squashed her eyebrows together. "Yes. She asked me what the police told us to do after I called."

"Right," Kelly said, with a nod. She noted Abby's name and that she had been in the room. "Do you remember where she was in the room?"

"She was…" Jodi paused as she searched her memory. "Near the fireplace."

"Okay, so she could have means and opportunity. She was near enough to the knife to grab it."

"But she'd have to dart across the room, stab Pearl, and go back."

"Easy enough – the lights were off for long enough."

"Were they though?"

"How long do you think they were off?" Kelly inquired.

"Two minutes," Jodi ventured.

Kelly scrunched up her lips. "That's a long time, though. Like, longer than you think."

Jodi tapped around on her phone.

"What are you doing?" Kelly asked.

"I'm going to time it."

"Okay. Oh, while you're in there, what time did you place the 9-1-1 call?"

"Ummm." Jodi tapped around again. "I placed the call at 8:46 p.m."

"Okay," Kelly said, as she jotted it at the top of the page and circled it three times.

Jodi frowned at her phone. "What?" Kelly asked.

"It's been like twenty-five seconds."

"See, I told you! Two minutes is a really long time!"

"Okay, so the power was off for at least ninety seconds. That just seems like such a short time for someone to grab a knife across the room and kill someone!"

"Which means we may be able to rule some people out based on where they were in the room."

"It seems like we can rule everyone out in that time frame. Were they running?"

Kelly's eyebrows shot up and her muscles stiffened. "Someone ran past me! They bumped into me."

"By accident on account of the darkness, or like they were rushing to grab the knife and kill someone?"

"It could have been either. It was pretty forceful. Maybe the latter? Oh, and what if someone pocketed the knife *before* the lights went out?"

"Oh, that could change everything."

"I think it's totally possible someone could grab the knife and get to Pearl then retreat to another area of the room in ninety seconds. But if they had the knife already–"

"They could do it easily," Jodi agreed.

"Right."

"I'm not convinced ninety seconds is enough time."

"We need to test it," Kelly said.

"Seriously?"

"Yes! We need to know if we can rule anyone out based on where they were."

"I thought you didn't want to leave the room because there's a crazed murderer in the house."

"I didn't say crazed," Kelly retorted, as she hopped off the bed and donned her slippers. "And I think we need to establish a time frame."

"Fine," Jodi said. "I'm not the one terrified to leave my room."

"I didn't say terrified," Kelly answered, wrapping her robe around her and tying it tight.

"Close enough," Jodi said.

CHAPTER 9

Kelly tugged the door open and glanced up and down the hall. "Coast's clear!" she whispered.

Jodi rolled her eyes as they stepped into the hall. "I thought you didn't want to go down those stairs again?"

"Ugh," Kelly groaned, dropping her head between her shoulders. "Those stairs. They're going to *kill* me before the end of this weekend."

"Oh, bad choice of words."

"You're right," Kelly said with a wince. "Either way, no, I'd rather not go down those stairs again, but duty calls."

"Duty?" Jodi repeated, her lips curling up with the words. "It's not on you to solve this."

"It kind of is on me to clear my name."

"Oh my gosh, Kelly, no one really thinks you did it!"

"Either way, I'd like to be prepared."

They emerged from the halls and Kelly stared down the many steps. Her shoulders slumped and she took a deep inhale before she circled her finger in the air. "Let's go."

They lumbered down the steps with Kelly groaning most of the way. "Why would *anyone* put this many stairs?"

"High ceilings," Jodi answered.

"*This* high?"

"Didn't you see those things? They're like fifteen feet high, easily!"

Kelly sighed as they reached the end. "Whew, I'm glad we don't own this place! I love our normal height ceilings."

"Oh come on, you don't want a house with a carousel in it?" Jodi asked as they entered the sitting room.

Kelly shrugged as she scanned the room. "Okay, Pearl was there." She pointed to the couch. "Knife was there." She swung her arm across to point at the table and narrowed her eyes at it. "Got your timer?"

"Yep," Jodi answered.

"Okay, I'll start over here, near the table." Kelly strode to a spot near the fireplace. "Start the timer."

Jodi tapped and said, "Okay."

Kelly hurried across the room, pretending to grab a knife. She raced to the couch, shoved it into the imaginary Pearl, and retreated to a spot near the fireplace.

"Time?"

"Forty-seven seconds."

"Okay, doable. Let's try another."

She crossed the room closer to the screen. This trial took a similar amount of time.

"Try one from across the room," Jodi suggested.

Kelly blew out a long breath. "You try one."

"I can't."

"Why not?"

"Because it'll bias the data. I'm a different speed than you," Jodi said.

"I'm a different speed than all the other people in the room, too, so what?"

"It's best to keep everything the same."

Kelly made a face. "Ugh, you're such a wuss."

"I'm doing the smart work," Jodi claimed.

"Right," Kelly said, as she positioned herself across the room. She sped past the couch, grabbed the imaginary knife, stabbed thin air while pretending it was Pearl, and hurried back to her spot.

"Sixty-five seconds," Jodi reported.

"So, basically everyone had means and opportunity," Kelly said with a sigh, as she stalked to the couch and sank onto it.

"Ew, you're sitting in the dead person's spot."

Kelly leapt up and winced, wiping off her robe as though she'd catch cooties.

"And probably, yes, everyone could have done it. Especially since we didn't consider they could have started and ended in different places."

Kelly rolled her eyes. "So, this was a waste."

"Well, not really."

"How do you figure that?"

"You probably burned off all the calories from your ice cream."

"Very funny, Jodi," Kelly said with a groan. "Let's go back up and continue making our list.'

"Okay. You sure you don't need a breather before we tackle those stairs?"

"I'd rather get it over with. If I sit down again, I may not move."

They left the sitting room, crossed the foyer, and, with heaving breaths, scaled the mountainous staircase.

Kelly puffed out a long breath as they reached the top. "I don't even want to know how many more times we'll have to climb those."

They wound through the halls and arrived back at Jodi's door. Kelly locked the door behind them after they pushed inside. Jodi slogged to the bed and climbed on top, kicking off her slippers then sliding under the covers.

Kelly tested the doors before joining Jodi, jiggling them back and forth to be sure they held tight. After she slid under the covers, she pulled her notebook onto her lap again.

"Okay, list of people. So far, I have Melissa and Abby."

"And Abby could have done it," Jodi noted.

"Right," Kelly said, jotting it down. "As could everyone else in the room. Which also included–" Kelly paused for a moment in thought. "Harper!"

Kelly scribbled the name on her notepad. "She definitely was there because she accused me of killing Pearl."

"Wait, was she? Or did she come in and accuse you?"

Kelly scrunched her face in thought. "She was there."

Jodi nodded. "You're right, she was."

"And she had means and opportunity."

"Like everyone in the room."

"Except us."

"Right, except us," Jodi agreed.

"But did Harper have motive?"

Jodi's lips puckered as she formed a response, her eyes narrowing. "Nnnnnoooo," she said slowly.

"Are we sure?"

"What motive would she have?"

"You're right. She's Melissa's friend. So, why would she care if Melissa's mother is dead or alive?"

"Unless she killed her *for* Melissa."

"Ohh!" Kelly said, her eyebrows shooting toward her hairline. "An accomplice."

"No, the killer. Melissa is the accomplice."

"Are you sure?" Kelly asked. "Cause I was thinking Melissa is like the mastermind and Harper is the accomplice."

"She's only an accomplice if she's planning it with her, but isn't the killer."

"Well, okay, whatever – we're getting wrapped up in

details that don't matter. Harper was there. She had means and opportunity, and we have a plausible motive, even if it's more far-fetched than others. When we're done, we can order people in terms of how likely it is they did it."

"Kelly, I'll be asleep by then."

"Then we'll do it tomorrow," Kelly said. "Now, come on and give me more names."

"Uh, the sister, what's her name?"

"Oh, right. Reagan?"

"No, Reagan is Pearl's cousin."

"Right," Kelly answered, writing the name next. "Let's work on Reagan. I'll put the sister next and put her name down when we remember it."

"Reagan was there," Jodi said.

"And so was her daughter, Audrey."

"Aubrey," Kelly corrected.

"Right."

"They both helped me with Pearl's sister when she went limp."

"They came from near the table," Jodi said. Her eyes grew wide. "They came from by the table!" she repeated, excitement in her voice.

"Yes!" Kelly shouted. "Yes, they did! We were nearer the armchair I put what's-her-name in, and they came from further across."

"Either of them could have done it, then!"

Kelly nodded and noted it on the paper. "Means, motive *and* opportunity." Kelly jotted the final note on the paper.

"What's the motive?"

"Money! They're probably in the will."

"Okay, that's likely. Okay, yeah, put that down. Did we ever establish a motive for Harper?"

"Yes. Killed Pearl for Melissa whose motive is money. So, basically, her motive is friendship and money."

Jodi nodded. "Right."

"Okay, next. The sister. What's her name?" Kelly balled a fist and clunked it against her forehead.

"Julia!"

"Right! Julia! How could I forget? She's one of the only ones with a normal name!" Kelly jotted Julia's name on the page. "Judging by her reaction, I'd say she didn't do it."

"What if she's a phenomenal actress?"

Kelly puckered her lips in thought. "Okay, so she races across the room from her chair, grabs a knife, kills her sister… why?"

"Money."

Kelly jabbed the pen at Jodi. "Right, money! She races back to her location by the chair, then pretends to faint when the lights come up."

"Plausible."

"Okay, another one with means, motive, and opportunity."

"How many do we have?"

"Six, so far."

"And there were…" Jodi paused as she closed her eyes and counted, her lips moving as she did the math in her head. "Sixteen people here."

"Ten more to go! Open the popcorn."

Jodi nodded and pulled the bag open, setting it between them. "Let's try to get Melissa's friends done."

"Okay, we have Abby and Harper so far." Kelly grabbed a handful of the cheesy popcorn, tossing a piece in her mouth.

"Madison and Everly," Jodi said, reaching into the bag for a handful of the treat.

Kelly nodded as she wrote. "Everly is the one who thinks Melissa did it."

"But Madison doesn't."

"Both of them were in the room."

"So both had means and opportunity. Motive the same as the other friends."

"But Everly thinks Melissa did it, so she couldn't have right?" She popped another piece of popcorn into her mouth.

"Unless she's lying," Jodi said between pieces.

"True."

"Okay, so there's those two accounted for. What's the other friend? The redhead?"

"Aurora. She was there. She was with Melissa when she almost fainted."

"Okay," Kelly said, as she finished her writing, "that's all the friends."

"Ummm, Emily, the sister-in-law."

"Oh, definitely motive. She probably hates Pearl for having her husband's money."

"Are we sure it's not Pearl's money?"

"No, but still, in-laws are tough."

"Did she have means? She doesn't move too quick, and she uses a cane."

"Maybe she used the cane to get the knife? Or maybe she doesn't need the cane. She seemed to walk pretty well."

"Maybe. Well, put a question mark by means."

Kelly placed a large question mark in the means column next to Emily. "Done." She grabbed another handful of popcorn.

"Emily had a daughter."

"Penny," Kelly finished while she munched on a piece of popcorn. "And she has the good pearls, darling," Kelly said, fluttering her eyelashes and using a posh voice.

"Oh, well, actually that may matter. If Emily and Penny have money–"

"Less motive."

"Bingo," Jodi said, digging in the bag for more popcorn.

"I'll put a question mark on motive for them both.

Moving on. There was the girl next to me at the table, Kennedy."

"Family friend, right?"

"Yep. So, she wouldn't get money."

"And she's not a friend of Melissa's."

"No motive?"

"None that I can see."

"Okay, she's low on the list then. Means and opportunity like everyone else, but that's it."

"Peyton, Pearl's cousin-in-law."

"Okay, same as any other family member, except, she, too, is older so maybe not so quick. She was across the room."

"Making her less likely to be able to pull it off."

Kelly nodded and noted it on the sheet. "Three to go."

"The nieces, Parker, Addison, and Willow."

"Carbon copies except for Willow."

"Why?"

"Willow had a bad attitude. She seemed to hate it here and hate the family. She could have done it."

"Good point."

Kelly finished her notes and settled back in the pillows, tapping the end of the pen against her lips.

"What do we have?"

"A houseful of people who could have committed murder."

"Another waste," Jodi complained.

"Not necessarily. The two most likely culprits on here are Melissa and Willow."

"With Melissa topping the list."

"Yep. She has the most to gain from Pearl's death presumably. *And* Pearl was really nasty to her. Imagine living with that all the time."

"And Everly thinks she did it."

"Which says *a lot*." Kelly put a star next to Melissa's name. "Although Madison doesn't think she did it."

"But Everly was her roommate. Madison wasn't."

They stared at the sheet for a few more moments before they agreed to get some sleep.

"I am not going to sleep by myself in that other room," Kelly said, "so make room." She folded the bag of popcorn down and set it on the night table.

"Yeah, yeah. I figured," Jodi said as she slid down under the covers and switched off her light.

Kelly flicked off her light and eased back into the pillows. She stared at the ceiling as dim light filtered through the windows and lightning occasionally lit the room.

"Jodi," she whispered after twenty minutes. She received no answer.

"Pssst, Jodi!" she tried again.

"Ugh, what?"

"Are you awake?"

"I am now that you woke me up," Jodi groaned, as she rolled onto her back.

"Who do you really think did it?"

Jodi flung her arm over her eyes and groaned. "I don't know, Kelly, go to sleep."

"I can't sleep. I can't believe someone got murdered! I just keep seeing it over and over again."

"Well, stop thinking about it."

"I can't! Every time I close my eyes, I see Pearl sitting there with the knife in her chest."

"Hopefully the cops will show up tomorrow morning and deal with this."

"Do you think they'll let us go home?"

"Why not?"

"Well, they'll probably question us first, and then what if they hold us all here indefinitely?"

"Why would they hold us indefinitely?"

Kelly flipped on her side and propped her head up with her hand. "I don't know! It could happen. We destroyed evidence! What if we all get charged with obstruction of justice?"

"We couldn't leave the body sitting on the couch until the cops got here."

Kelly remained silent for a moment. "Who recommended we move the body?"

Jodi pulled her arm away from her eyes, her brow furrowing as she considered it. "That butler guy."

"Oh my gosh," Kelly exclaimed, "what if he did it?"

"He wasn't even there."

"Oh, did he come in after?"

"Yeah. At least I think so."

"Still, we're completely overlooking that the staff could have done this."

"I don't remember any of them being there."

"Well, they did bring the champagne, so they were there at some point. What if one of them hung around or slipped back in? It's not like we'd notice them that much."

"I guess it could have happened. What's their motive?"

"Being mad? Like hating Pearl because she was nasty to them? She seemed really unpleasant. Maybe it was some kind of revenge."

"I guess it's as plausible as any other theory we have," Jodi yawned. "But I still think we need to leave this to the police."

Kelly flopped back into the pillows, staring at the ceiling. After another thirty minutes of lying awake, she reached toward the night table. She eased the popcorn bag off the table and onto her lap. She pushed up to sit and quietly unfurled the bag. She winced with every squeak.

"I can hear that," Jodi mumbled.

"I'm hungry," Kelly admitted.

"How can you be hungry after all that ice cream?"

"I don't know! But I am. Don't judge." Kelly tossed a piece of popcorn into her mouth.

The bed jiggled as Jodi sat up and turned over. "The least you can do is share."

"Says the person who can't fathom how I'm hungry."

"I don't want to chance getting hungry after you finish eating because you kept me up."

Kelly waved the bag over as Jodi flicked on her light. They ate in silence for ten minutes before Jodi waved the bag away. "Think you can sleep now?"

"I hope so."

"Just stop thinking about it," Jodi said, as she squashed her pillow into a ball and slammed her head on it.

"Yeah, yeah, yeah," Kelly murmured, as she inched down and eased into her pillow. She blew out a long breath and closed her eyes. After pursing her lips following a number of loud booms of thunder, Kelly slipped off to sleep, pondering who may be a murderer.

CHAPTER 10

Kelly yawned and stretched the next morning. She rolled over, finding Jodi's side of the bed empty. Rain still pelted the large window to her left. Kelly ducked to view the sky, still filled with black clouds.

"Another beautiful day at Willow Lake," Kelly groaned.

Jodi popped out of the bathroom. "Oh, you're up! Good. I want to get to breakfast. I bet they put out an amazing spread."

"How can you think of eating? There's a dead woman in the freezer!"

"I doubt they keep the breakfast food in there."

"That's not what I meant."

"Just get dressed. I'm starving."

Kelly climbed from the bed with a groan and disappeared into the bathroom, passing through to grab a change of clothes from her bag before she completed her morning routine. She emerged into the bedroom, fully dressed.

Jodi leapt from the armchair. "Let's go!"

"Okay, okay, Jodi. I can't believe you're so interested in eating with these people. One of them is a killer!"

"Maybe breakfast this morning will tell us something," Jodi countered.

"How?" Kelly inquired, as they entered the hall.

"Maybe someone won't show up."

"And that makes them guilty?"

"No, but it may be telling. Would you come to breakfast if you just killed someone?"

"Maybe. To make it look good."

"Okay, so maybe the people at breakfast are more suspicious."

Kelly wiggled her eyebrows. "I guess maybe we'll find something out."

They descended the stairs and veered right toward the dining room. Kelly's eyes widened as they entered. Several ladies already milled around, retrieving food, or eating. A few spoke quietly to each other, the vibe definitely subdued compared to the night before.

Across the room, food filled the ten-foot buffet. Kelly patted Jodi's arm. "You were right, look at all that food!"

"Told you," Jodi whispered.

They wandered across the room, grabbing plates from the server. Kelly eyed several of the others in the room, offering a tight-lipped smile as people glanced at the pair of them.

"No Melissa," Kelly noted to Jodi. She spooned scrambled eggs onto her plate.

"That's understandable. Her mother's dead," Jodi answered, as she used tongs to load a few pieces of bacon onto her plate.

"Or she killed her."

"No Julia either," Jodi noted.

"Are those donuts?"

"Looks like it."

"I need another plate." Kelly circled back to grab a second

plate for the breakfast pastries. After placing two on the plate, she wandered toward the table with Jodi.

They found seats alone at the end. Kelly scanned the rest of the women. Abby, Everly, and Madison were seated together, speaking in hushed tones. Kennedy sat with Aubrey and Peyton. Most of Pearl's family members were missing, outside of her in-laws.

Kelly finished her food and dug into the glazed donut calling her name from the second plate. She bit into it, the gooey glaze melting on her tongue. "Mmm," she moaned with her mouth still full. "So good."

She shoved the donut in her mouth for a second bite. As she bit down, Harper entered the room. She scanned the space. Her eyebrows shot skyward as she focused on Kelly.

"You!" she shouted, as she shoved a finger in Kelly's direction.

Kelly's eyebrows inched up as her eyes shot side-to-side. With the donut still clamped between her lips, she pointed back to herself, her face questioning.

"Yes, Donut, you! How could you show your face here!" All eyes turned to Kelly.

Kelly bit off the chunk of donut and chewed as she shook her head. "What are you talking about?" she asked, after swallowing.

"You killed Pearl and then you come to breakfast like it's nothing?"

Kelly's eyes went wide, and she glanced at Jodi before flicking her gaze back to Harper. "I didn't kill her."

Harper narrowed her eyes and crossed her arms, stamping a high-heeled foot on the floor. "Prove it."

Kelly's brow furrowed, and her jaw dropped open. "What?"

"You heard me. Prove you didn't do it."

"Why would I kill her? I have no motive!"

Kennedy stood from the table. "Ladies, please. Let's take it down a notch."

"I agree," Jodi chimed in. "Let's let the police handle this."

Kennedy shook her head. "I spoke with the police this morning. Since the weather is still bad, they aren't going to make it for several hours, if at all today. But in the meantime, we have other business to take care of here."

"Yeah, like finding the real killer," Kelly said.

"Actually, there's something else," Kennedy answered. "And that's why I'm asking all of you to join me in the sitting room after your meal. Pearl is dead. And there is the matter of her estate to settle."

Madison guffawed. "Surely that can wait."

"These are Pearl's wishes."

"But Melissa will be far too upset to deal with that now," Madison retorted.

"I'm only doing what Pearl asked of me as her attorney."

Kelly shot Jodi a glance, her eyebrows shooting upward. "She's Pearl's attorney, not just a family friend," she murmured.

Jodi bobbed her head up and down discreetly. "I can't wait to find out who profits the most. It might help us."

"Especially with the police not coming."

Jodi wiped the corners of her mouth and nodded. The others had already begun to parade to the sitting room.

Kelly leapt from her seat. "I'm going to grab another donut and we can strategize how to get the information after they're finished."

Kennedy approached them. "Ladies, if you wouldn't mind joining us?"

"Oh," Kelly said, as she set a chocolate-filled powdered donut on her plate, "I don't think it's our place to be there. It's a private family matter."

"Actually, it concerns you very much," Kennedy said.

Kelly glanced at Jodi and raised her shoulders up. "Uh, well, okay." She waved the plate in the air and laughed. "Just grabbing one for the road."

Kennedy eyed her up and down, before spinning on her heel and strutting around the long table and out the door, her high heels clicking off the hardwood.

"What is that about?" Kelly whispered, as she grabbed her napkin and stuffed it under her plate.

Jodi shrugged. "I don't know. But I think I'll grab another donut, too."

"Well, hurry up. I don't want to miss why this somehow concerns us."

Jodi waved her comment away as she grabbed a jelly donut. She took a bite before setting it on the plate and licking her fingers.

"Maybe we need to be witnesses or something," Kelly suggested.

They skirted the table and strode down the hall, each polishing off half of their donuts on the way. They entered the sitting room, plates in hand. A group of four women consisting of Madison, Aurora, Everly, and Harper hovered over Melissa, who sat in an armchair, clutching a tissue.

"I can't believe she's gone," Melissa choked out.

Harper spotted Kelly and Jodi and narrowed her eyes. "How dare you come here!"

"Easy, Harper," Kennedy said, as she strutted across the room, a remote in her hand. "I asked them to come."

"Why?" Willow inquired. She slouched on the couch, her arms crossed over her loose-fitting hoodie covering her top half and down to the thighs of her pajama pants.

Julia sank into an armchair across the room. Her shoulders slumped forward and shook as she sobbed.

The others milled around the room, everyone avoiding

the spot Pearl had sat in last night when she was murdered. A few stragglers, including Abby, Parker, and Penelope strolled in.

Reagan sat on a bench in front of the grand piano tucked into a corner of the room. Aubrey leaned against the colossal object like a lounge singer. Penelope hurried toward them and hugged them both. Her mother, Emily, joined them, leaving her seat on one of the room's chaises.

A few other family members grouped around Julia as Kennedy stood near the projector screen which had played the montage of photos of Pearl less than twenty-four hours ago.

"Ladies, if you please," Kennedy shouted.

The hushed conversations across the room ground to a halt.

Kennedy continued, "As many of you know, I am Pearl's attorney."

Reagan waved her hand in the air to stop Kennedy. "I'm sorry, Ms. Moore, but is this really necessary? Pearl died less than twenty-four hours ago. We're all still grieving."

"And shouldn't we wait for Pearl's other family?" Peyton asked.

"Yeah, like the males in the family, specifically?" Willow offered.

Kennedy pursed her lips and nodded before waving her hands in the air to stop the barrage of questions. "Ladies, please. This meeting stems directly from Pearl's request."

"She couldn't have known that when she died the estate would be inaccessible by most family," Parker said.

Kennedy drew in a deep breath and licked her lips before she spoke. "Actually, Pearl made recent updates to her will."

Gasps sounded throughout the room.

"And," Kennedy continued, "she gave me specific instructions for what to do in the event that she did not live beyond this party."

"What?" Julia choked out.

"Are you saying Pearl specifically told you she thought she might die this weekend?" Penny asked.

"I'm saying," Kennedy answered, "Pearl gave me specific instructions about her wishes in the event that she did not survive this weekend."

"And those were?" Aubrey asked.

"I'll let Pearl tell you herself," Kennedy said, motioning toward the screen behind her.

Kennedy pressed a button, and a blue screen sprang to life on the white canvas. Within moments, a frozen image of Pearl formed on the screen.

"Seriously?" Willow asked.

"Can someone get the lights?" Kennedy asked, her finger hovering over the large center button on the remote.

Closest to the door, Kelly dimmed the lights. Kennedy pointed the remote toward the screen and pressed a button.

Pearl's form sprang to life. "Is it ready?" she asked someone off-camera.

An incoherent response sounded off-screen, and Pearl nodded, directing her gaze to the camera.

She shrugged her shoulders and spoke in her gruff tone. "Well, if you're seeing this, I'm dead."

A sob escaped from Melissa, and she leaned forward, sinking her head into her hands.

"Is this really necessary?" Everly questioned.

As if in response, Pearl continued, "I'm sure you're each all broken up over my death." She let out a harsh cackle. "No, you're not. What you're really wondering is who's going to get all my money. Will it be Melissa? Will I dole it out dollar by dollar to all of you?

"And I'm sure one of you already complained about having the menfolk here." On-screen, Pearl rolled her eyes.

"The truth is," she continued, "it doesn't matter. You can play it for them later if you want. Though I doubt you'll want to. You'll be busy lawyering up and storming the courts."

"What is she talking about?" Parker shouted.

Kennedy waved her hand to hush the woman.

"Here's the rub. I can't stand any of you. Male or female. And since someone at this little shindig just offed me, I hate you women more. One of you killed me. And the rest of you let it happen."

Gasps rang out at the admission from Pearl. "There's my dear sister, Julia, who's probably weeping in an armchair right now. Where were you when I needed your help all those years ago, Julia? Hmmm? Can't answer? I'll bet you can't."

"Then there are my in-laws. You hated me from the time William married me.

"And all my lovely nieces. Weak, sniveling little brats, every last one of you. Spoiled simple. Think the world owes you. Well, I don't.

"And last but not least, my supposedly loving daughter, Melissa. Don't think I don't know what you're doing, Melissa. With your loving little montages at every party in the hopes of winning every last cent from me. And your little hanger-on friends, hoping to cash in on your gravy train.

"You all make me sick!" Pearl's face formed an ugly frown, and she shook her head. She gritted her teeth, her jaw clenched. She sucked in a deep breath before continuing.

"And that's why I'm not leaving my money to anyone of you."

Pearl shrugged and wobbled her head around. "Well, almost none of you."

On-screen, Pearl chuckled. Her laughter turned into a full-blown cackle, and she clapped her hands.

"So, who is she leaving it to?" someone shouted, though Kelly couldn't identify the voice.

"Have they started to ask who I'm leaving it to yet, Kennedy?" Pearl inquired. "Has anyone demanded justice?" Pearl waved her fist in the air. "Have they already threatened to have the will overturned?"

Pearl continued her chuckling for a few more seconds before the giggles died off. A grin remained on her lips. "And now you're all wondering who the lucky winner is!"

Kelly took a bite of her donut as Pearl's eyes focused on the camera.

"Since I hate all of you, I'm leaving the entire estate, money, and everything to the last person I met. I don't care who it is – a waiter, a maid, someone from the streets. Kennedy's keeping a list. She knows who it is. Good luck to that person. The rest of you can stew in your own juices. And before you start your challenges, I'm of sound mind and body. I know what I'm doing. So you can all go to he…"

The video glitched and froze before the final syllable played.

"What the hell was that?" a voice said. Again, Kelly didn't see who the speaker was. Penny twisted the knob on the wall, bringing the lights up. Everyone squinted against them as the bickering continued.

"She has to be kidding!" another woman shouted. "She's kidding, right?"

"She was not. The official will was changed and filed over one month ago." Kennedy waved a thick set of papers in the air.

"This cannot be legal!" Emily yelled.

"I assure you it is," Kennedy said.

Kelly raised her eyebrows at Jodi as she bit into the last quarter of her donut.

"Well, who is the last person she met? Who's inheriting everything?"

Kennedy licked her lips, her gaze flicking across the room. All eyes followed hers, landing on Kelly.

CHAPTER 11

Kelly froze mid-bite as she became the center of attention. A few of the ladies stood. Melissa's friends glared at her. Aurora crossed her arms and narrowed her eyes at her. Julia's lower lip trembled.

Addison threw her arms in the air. "You're kidding?"

Willow burst into laughter at the turn of events, doubling over with giggles.

Kelly set the remaining bit of donut on the plate and chewed the wad in her mouth. "Me?" she questioned, with her mouth full.

"Technically, she met both you and your sister at the same time," Kennedy answered, "but who's counting?"

"As if you didn't know," Harper said, stamping her foot on the ground, her hand resting on her cocked hip.

Kelly gulped down the donut. "How could I know?" Kelly exclaimed.

"You knew! And you killed her!"

"That's crazy!"

"Your powdered sugar fingerprints are all over this," Harper snarked.

Kelly glanced at her fingers and then rubbed them on her napkin. "This is ridiculous. I'd never met Pearl before yesterday. How could I possibly know this?"

"Seems like you've worked it out pretty nicely for yourself," Aurora said.

"Again, how could I have known this?"

"It doesn't matter," Melissa said, standing from her armchair. She sniffed once, flicking away a tear, her face set in stone. "It'll never hold up in court."

She stalked toward the door, flicking her gaze toward Kelly, her eyes filled with contempt. "You'll never own Willow Lake."

She pushed past Kelly, knocking her back a step as she skirted through the door. Her posse of college friends followed her in short order, each of them glowering at Kelly and Jodi.

Reagan and Aubrey grouped around Julia. "Come on, Aunt Julia," Aubrey said, helping the woman from the chair. "I think we've heard enough."

"We'll talk in private about what to do," Reagan said. Together, she and Aubrey led the grieving woman from the room. Aubrey shook her head at Kelly.

Kelly's jaw fell open and she scrunched up her face as she glanced at Jodi.

The remaining women stood speechless, most of them still focused on Kelly. Kennedy addressed what was left of the group. "That's all I have for you ladies. Kelly, Jodi, I'll be in touch once this horrible weekend is over. In the meantime, if you have any questions, feel free to ask. I have some of my paperwork with me, so I can give you general specifics."

Kennedy shoved the papers she'd been holding into a briefcase sitting on the floor under the screen and grabbed it by the handle. She stalked from the room, handing her card off to a stunned Kelly and Jodi.

* * *

Kelly and Jodi pushed through the doors leading to Jodi's room. Kelly still wore the stunned expression she'd had in the sitting room. Not even the mountain of stairs had removed it from her face.

She eased the doors shut and leaned against them, her mind moving in a hundred different directions at once. Across the room, Jodi paced the floor as she turned Kennedy's card over and over in her hands.

"I can't believe this," Kelly finally choked out.

Jodi stopped her pacing and glanced at Kelly. "Do you think we heard right?"

Kelly cocked her head. "Yeah, I'd say we did. Kennedy said we're the ones inheriting all Pearl's loot. And now everyone hates us even more than they already did when they thought all I did was kill the woman."

"It can't be real!" Jodi said, flopping onto the bed.

"No, I can't believe it'll hold up in court. I think Melissa's correct on that point. All this does is muddy the waters. We have no new evidence as to who may have killed Pearl."

"Could you imagine how different our lives would be if it was?"

"Jodi," Kelly replied, with a frown, "be serious. We're never going to inherit this place. And that's probably for the best."

Jodi wrinkled her forehead at Kelly. "How do you figure that?"

"Someone died here!"

"So what?" Jodi said with a shrug. "I'm pretty sure all the other perks outweigh that. No more money troubles."

"We don't have money troubles," Kelly said, slumping into the armchair.

"We sort of do."

"We get by."

"No more getting by," Jodi corrected. "We could travel like we always wanted to."

Kelly shrugged as she considered it.

"And imagine all the pearl parties we could host here."

"Why would we host pearl parties? We won't need to work."

"Well, we could work for fun. You know, to supplement or give it to charity or whatever." Jodi leapt from the bed and paced the floor again. Her eyes lit up and she pointed a finger at Kelly. "And… carousel room."

"The carousel room may be worth it, I'll admit, but at what cost, Jodi? Think of climbing those stairs daily."

"I'll make the sacrifice."

"Well, my knees may not."

"I'll buy you a chairlift."

"Forget that – we'll put in a fancy elevator." She sighed before continuing. "It's never going to happen. We'll probably get sued six ways from Sunday by every person in this house, *and* I'll go to jail for killing Pearl."

"The police can't possibly believe that story. Why would you kill her?"

"Uh, because apparently, we're inheriting a fortune."

"How could we have known that?"

"Maybe Kennedy told us at dinner. And then I killed her to make sure I was the last person she met."

"OMG," Jodi exclaimed, pausing in her pacing. "Did she tell you?"

"No! Jodi! I'm just saying as a for instance. But that's exactly my point. Even you're starting to question if I knew. Imagine being the police. They could totally buy that story."

"I wonder if I'd still inherit if you went to jail."

"Jodi!" Kelly shouted at her. "We have to figure this out, so I don't!"

"Sorry! I'm just trying to find a silver lining if this goes south."

"Oh, I'll bet. You can just hang out here, riding the unicorn in the carousel room while I serve twenty to life."

"Was there a unicorn?"

Kelly's shoulders slumped and she tilted her head, a frown forming on her lips.

"Okay, sorry. But I don't see how we're going to solve this. We have no new information, and now everyone hates you, so they won't tell us anything."

"I'm pretty sure everyone hates both of us. They just hate me more, because they think I also killed Pearl."

Kelly mulled over the information. She stalked across the room, grabbed her notepad, and studied the list they'd made last night. "All these motives primarily depend on money. We have to figure out what Pearl's will said before she changed it. Maybe that'll help us."

"How are we going to do that?"

"Maybe we should ask Kennedy."

"Do you think she'll tell us?"

"We can try."

"How are we going to find her?"

"Call her, duh!" Kelly said, waving the business card around in the air. She pulled her phone from the pocket of her cardigan and punched in the number.

"Put it on speaker," Jodi whispered.

Kelly nodded and clicked the speakerphone button. The line trilled four times before they received a message about leaving a voicemail. Kelly ended the call.

"Why did you do that? You should have left a message."

"And say what? Hey, Kennedy, this is Kelly. I'm just trying

to figure out who killed Pearl since I didn't do it, and wondered if you could tell me who should have inherited Pearl's money?"

"No," Jodi said, rolling her eyes. "Just say you had a few questions and wondered if we could speak in private."

"Oh." Kelly puckered her lips, considering it. "That's kinda good. Okay, wait, I'll call back and leave a message."

Kelly dialed the number, and the phone rang again. She waited through the four rings before the recorded message played. Kelly bobbed her head and motioned with her hand for the message to hurry. When the beep sounded, Kelly went into her spiel, ending with a "thanks, bye!" before ending the call.

Jodi plopped onto the bed and crossed her legs at her ankles. "Okay, I guess we'll wait for her to call back."

Kelly paced the floor, biting her thumbnail. "I can't relax. Isn't there something else we can do?"

"Like what?"

Kelly shrugged as she continued to pace. "Go search a file cabinet or something?"

Jodi narrowed her eyes as she considered the suggestion. "Okay."

Kelly ceased her pacing and stared at her sister. "Seriously?"

"Well, we can explore the house. It's ours now."

"Be serious, Jodi," Kelly said. "We'll never actually inherit it. Melissa is bound and determined to make sure we don't."

"Either way, right now, we're inheriting this place. So, we have every right to check it out. Like a home inspection."

"Good enough excuse for me. That's what we'll tell anyone we run into."

"Yeah," Jodi said, as she pulled the door open. "They already hate us. We may as well give them even more reason to."

"Do you think they'll cancel all their orders?"

"Does it matter?"

Kelly meandered down the hall next to Jodi. "If we don't inherit this place, it might."

"I guess we'll cross that bridge if we come to it. I didn't see an office downstairs when we were wandering around, but that's where it would be, right?"

"I didn't see one either, but we probably didn't go everywhere."

"I guess we'll start down there, then."

"Oh, the stairs," Kelly lamented as they reached the top.

They descended them and stood in the foyer, spinning in a slow circle to scan the space. Jodi shoved her hands into the back pockets of her jeggings and scrunched up her face in thought. "Well, we know the sitting room is through there."

"And that doesn't have any file cabinets."

"The dining room is that way," Kelly said, pointing toward the hall opposite the sitting room.

"Maybe we can try the hall back there." Jodi pointed to a hallway tucked behind the staircase.

"Okay," Kelly said.

They rounded the staircase and approached the hallway. A voice stopped them in their tracks.

"Didn't take you two long to start playing queens of the manor."

Kelly slowly spun around to face the speaker. Parker stood in the foyer, her arms folded over her chest and a sour expression on her face.

"That's not what we're doing," Kelly said.

"Really? It wasn't enough that Pearl's dead and you've stolen *our* inheritance, but you've got to rub it in? Why don't you take a spin past the carousel room and take a victory ride?"

"We just might," Jodi said, matching Parker's stance and narrowing her eyes at the woman.

"Jodi!" Kelly warned through clenched teeth.

"You two are real pieces of work. You won't get away with this!"

With that statement, Parker spun on her heel and stomped her way across the foyer, disappearing down the hall leading to the dining room.

Kelly guffawed, flinging her arms out. "Why does everyone act like we had some hand in this? We had nothing to do with this."

"I'm pretty sure we're not the most popular people in the house right now, under the circumstances. Come on, let's try to find the office."

They returned to their plan, turning back toward the back hall, and starting down it. Jodi poked her head into the first door in the hallway. She shook her head as she stepped out.

"Do you think Harper could be guilty?"

Jodi shrugged. "Why her?"

"She's so acrid toward us. She can't let it go."

"So?"

"So what if she's deflecting? She's pointing the finger at us to take suspicion off of her?"

"I suppose that's possible," Jodi answered, as she checked another room. "Library."

"Do you think there'd be something in there?" Kelly asked.

"We can take a look around."

"Let's see what books are in our new library," Kelly said, with a wink.

They stepped into the large space. Two floor-to-ceiling windows stood across the room sandwiched between equally large mahogany bookcases. Kelly took a few steps into the room, spinning to take it all in. A fireplace stood against the far wall, leather armchairs surrounding it.

Kelly ran her hand along the curved wooden banister of a spiraling staircase leading to the gallery above with yet more bookcases.

"How long do you think it would take to read all these?" Kelly asked, as she scanned volume after volume packing the shelves.

"More time than we have."

"Not if we have the rest of our lives."

"We'd still never make it through these."

Kelly stepped on the circular staircase. "I'll take a look around up here."

"Okay," Jodi said, as she wandered around the lower level.

Kelly climbed the rounded staircase and stepped onto the second level. She ran her fingers along the white and mahogany banister as she wandered down the suspended gallery. No files or file cabinets graced this level. Nothing more than books.

Kelly wrapped her hands around the banister and leaned against it. She stared out the window across from her before scanning the floor below. Jodi stood over a book on a podium in the corner.

"Can you imagine having this library in your *home?*"

Jodi glanced up at Kelly. "Amazing," Jodi said. "Though I doubt it will be ours."

"Losing faith already?" Kelly questioned.

Jodi pointed to the book. "This is the family bible. It tracks the Willow family for generations."

"So?" Kelly made her way back to the spiral stairs and descended them.

"So, they didn't keep this in the family for all this time to give it away to two pearl pushers because Pearl was being a b–"

"What are you two doing in here?" a voice asked.

Kelly and Jodi spun to face the room's newest occupant. Willow stood at the door.

"Just looking around," Kelly said with a shrug. "Killing time."

She squeezed her eyes shut as she realized her terrible choice of words.

"Interesting choice of words," Willow said. "Killing time checking out the house you're about to inherit from a woman killed with your own knife."

Kelly sighed, slumping her shoulders before launching into a tirade about her innocence. Before she could, Willow continued. "Don't get me wrong, I don't think you did it. But I'm probably in the minority. And I couldn't care less if you take this pile of bricks. I don't want it."

"Really?" Jodi asked. "Why?"

"I don't want anything from Pearl Willow Barlow."

She turned on a heel and stalked from the room.

"Wow, someone has a real problem with Pearl," Kelly said. "Do you think she could have done it?"

"I wouldn't be surprised," a new voice said.

Kelly spun to identify the next person entering the library. Penelope sashayed into the room. She stalked to the drink cart in the corner nearest the door and poured herself a drink. She sipped it as she sauntered to the window and gazed out.

"Care to explain that?" Kelly inquired, after a moment.

Penelope shrugged. "Willow is… complicated. And she has every reason to hate Pearl."

Kelly's eyebrows raised and she shot Jodi a glance.

"Why's that?" Jodi asked.

"Pearl is responsible for her mother's death."

CHAPTER 12

"What?" Kelly asked, shock apparent in her voice.

Penelope twisted to face them with a coy smile on her lips.

"How?" Jodi added.

"Yeah, how is Pearl responsible for Willow's mother's death?" Kelly echoed.

"Penny, that's enough," Emily said, from the doorway.

"It's the truth," Penelope said to her mother with a shrug.

"It's not a subject to be aired at random." Emily flicked her gaze from Kelly to Jodi. "Perhaps you ladies should be on your way."

"Wait a minute, I think we have a right to know what she meant," Kelly argued. "Everyone is accusing me of killing Pearl, but I didn't do it. Someone else did, and I think we should figure out who!"

"Penny's said enough. She's spoken out of turn. Willow isn't the guilty party. Now, move along."

Jodi grabbed hold of Kelly's arm and tugged her toward the door. "Come on, Kelly. Let's just go."

Kelly began to object, but Jodi shot her a glance warning her otherwise. Kelly gave in, following Jodi into the hall. With a curt smile, Emily closed the doors behind them as they stepped out.

"Jodi!" Kelly said, as she continued down the hall. "Penny just accused Willow of murder, and you thought we should leave it?"

"We have the information we need. We have a new motive. And Willow is a wild card. We should look into it further."

"That's what I was trying to do, when you insisted we leave!"

"No, you were getting Penny's side of the story. That doesn't mean it's true."

"So, what do you propose we do? Ask Willow?"

"Maybe," Jodi said, with a shrug.

"Seriously? Are we supposed to just say, 'Hey, Willow, heard Pearl was responsible for your mom's death? Did you kill her?'?"

"No, but–" Jodi glanced into another room. "Bingo! Office!"

"Maybe we'll find something in here. Though I still think we should have just pursued that lead with Penny."

"We can ask any family member. I'll bet they all know. Emily wasn't going to let her say anything else. We'll have to follow it up another way."

They stepped into the small office space. Two file cabinets stood next to the door leading inside. Another stood on the adjacent wall.

"I'll check these two," Kelly said. "You try that one and the desk."

Jodi crossed the room and pawed through the drawers of the desk. Kelly pulled open one of the filing cabinets and scanned the folders.

"This is all house stuff."

"Oh, good. We'll know where to find it when we move in."

"Ha! Right."

Kelly tried another drawer, finding nothing of interest. She tugged at the bottom drawer.

"Locked. See if there's a key in the desk."

Jodi plopped onto the desk chair with a handful of pictures she'd found in a drawer. "Okay."

Kelly scanned the next file cabinet, but it contained nothing of interest. "Did you find a key?"

"Not yet," Jodi answered, still shuffling through pictures.

"What did you find?" Kelly wandered over and glanced over her shoulder. "Are these Melissa?"

"Yeah. They were in the bottom drawer."

"Wait, go back," Kelly said, as Jodi flipped through them.

Jodi flicked back through the pictures. "There, that one," Kelly said.

The picture showed a young girl standing in a pink leotard and tutu. Ballet shoes were strapped to her feet. She posed in first position. "That's not Melissa."

"No, it's not," Jodi said. She flipped the picture over, but it had no name or identifying marks.

"Who is that?"

"Doesn't say."

"And why is that picture mixed in with Melissa's?"

"I don't know."

"Give it to me." Kelly swiped the picture from the stack and shoved it in her cardigan pocket. "Did you find a key yet?"

"No." Jodi rummaged through a few other drawers. She pulled a small key from the bottom of one. "Aha!"

Kelly smiled at her and swiped the key from between her thumb and index finger. She hurried to the file cabinet and unlocked the bottom drawer.

Jodi followed her. "Is there a will in there?"

"No," Kelly said, her shoulders slumping. "Just a few checks and ledgers."

"Useless," Jodi said, as Kelly slid the drawer closed.

They searched through the other two file cabinets, but found nothing of importance.

"I guess we'll move on," Kelly said, as she climbed to her feet.

They traversed through the halls, searching for any additional rooms that might contain a copy of the previous will. Unfortunately, they found nothing outside of another few sitting rooms, a movie theater, a bowling alley, a ballroom, and a sunroom with a patio.

Rain still fell steadily from the sky, making it impossible for them to enjoy any fresh air outside. Kelly crossed her arms as she stared at the gray clouds above through the floor-to-ceiling windows.

"What a weekend," she murmured.

"Let's keep going."

Kelly nodded and followed Jodi into the hall. "Can you imagine if we did inherit this place? I'll throw a hip out just trying to get to all the rooms we have."

"Could you imagine the pearl parties we could throw, though? Weekend long events complete with movies, bowling, amusement park rides, and more!"

They rounded a corner into the hallway with the lazy river. "Oh, let's take a ride on the carousel," Jodi said.

"We may as well. It may be the last time we get to ride a carousel in a house. I don't think we'll be invited back after this. And I still don't believe we'll actually inherit this place."

Jodi chuckled at the statement. They found the large doors to the carousel room and tugged them open. The calliope wound up and music filled the air. Horses bobbed up and down as the platform spun to life.

Kelly and Jodi stepped onto the spiraling platform, careful to keep their balance before selecting their steeds. This time, Kelly chose a jet-black horse posed in full gallop, while Jodi climbed onto a gray horse with its black tail flicking in the unseen breeze.

They bobbed up and down for a few moments as the music played before Kelly spoke.

"Do you think Willow did it?" she shouted over the music.

"Do you?" Jodi answered.

"You shouldn't answer a question with a question."

"I thought Melissa was our most likely suspect?"

"Because of the money?"

"Don't answer a question with a question."

"If we could find out if Melissa was the sole or largest heir in a previous version of the will, we may have something," Kelly said, pushing a lock of hair from her face as it blew across from her ride. "But Penny seemed sure it was Willow."

"Harper seems sure it's you. That doesn't make you guilty."

"No, and it's because I'm not guilty that we need to take some of these accusations seriously. Someone did it. And our two most likely suspects are Melissa and Willow."

"I wonder how Pearl was responsible for her mother's death."

"Maybe we can Google it when we get back to our room."

"What are you going to search? How did Pearl kill Willow's mom?"

"No, duh. We'll search for Willow's mother's obituary and see what it says."

Jodi shrugged as she climbed from her horse. "Maybe we'll find something out."

Kelly sighed as she dismounted from her horse and they exited, closing the room off behind them. "I'd rather ride around on the carousel all day."

"Me too," Jodi admitted.

"But the stairs call." Kelly glanced into the distance, a sad expression on her face.

"Too bad we didn't find an elevator."

"How did Pearl do this every day?"

"I guess she was used to it."

They reached the massive staircase and started their trek to the second floor. They wound through the halls to their bedrooms.

Jodi flung the door open to her room and stepped inside. A crinkling noise sounded. She stumbled forward, glancing behind her to find what caused her to trip.

A manila envelope lay just inside the doorway. Kelly snatched it from the floor. "What's this?"

"A tripping hazard," Jodi complained.

Kelly stepped inside with the thick, unmarked envelope and closed the door. She glanced at Jodi, who was hunched over, rubbing her ankle through her boot. "Did you twist it?"

"It's fine," she said, after a moment. "I just stepped wrong on it. What's in that?"

"I don't know," Kelly said. She flipped over the envelope and studied the back. No marks graced either side. "Guess I'll open it."

She tore open the flap and glanced inside. Jodi lifted her chin, peering over the edge. "What's in it?"

Kelly slid out a variety of papers. A few loose papers fluttered to the floor. Jodi retrieved them.

"There's a note."

"What's it say?" Jodi asked, peering over Kelly's shoulder as she read aloud.

"If you want to help your sister, here's everything you need. Melissa did this. Use the information inside to make sure she pays for it."

CHAPTER 13

*J*odi's jaw dropped as Kelly flipped the note over, but found no signature on either side of the paper scrap.

She shuffled through the rest of the papers. "There's a copy of the will here." Kelly paged through it as she sank onto the bed. "It names Melissa as the primary heir. She gets the house, almost all of the money, and everything Pearl owns!"

"Wow, when is that dated?"

"Ummm," Kelly searched through the pages, finding signatures and dates, "Six months ago."

Jodi's eyebrows raised. "So, as recently as six months ago, Melissa thought she was getting the whole shebang."

"Seems so," Kelly said, as she scanned through the rest of the will.

"Which is an excellent reason to kill someone."

"But your own mother?" Kelly questioned. "What are those?" She motioned toward the papers in Jodi's hand which had fluttered to the floor.

Jodi scanned the sheets. "Printouts of text messages," she

murmured as she studied them.

"Text messages?"

Jodi nodded and Kelly stood, circling around her to peer at the pages.

"There are no names other than Melissa Barlow at the top. Whoever this was was talking to Melissa."

Jodi read them aloud: "*No idea. She frustrates me so much. Sometimes I could just... kill her.*"

Jodi shuffled to the next page. "*Honestly, I cannot wait for her to kick it. She's such a monster.*"

Yet another page detailed another nasty message about her mother, this one naming Pearl. "*The earth will be a better place when Pearl Barlow is gone.*"

"Wow," Kelly mumbled.

"Really. Talk about issues with your mother."

"She really hated her," Kelly agreed.

"But did she hate her enough to kill her?"

"Money's a strong motivator. And she was set to inherit everything. And did you notice how different she acted when she found out she wasn't inheriting? Her tears dried up like that." Kelly snapped her fingers. "And she was in fight mode."

"Coping mechanism?"

"Would you care right after your mother was murdered? She went from grieving to hostile in two seconds flat."

Jodi puckered her lips and considered it. She stared down at the papers in her hand. "The evidence does seem to be against her."

"Should we show this to Kennedy?"

"Why her?" Jodi asked.

"Why not? She's handling Pearl's estate."

"What if she sent this?"

"Maybe she sent it to see if we'd turn Melissa in."

Jodi's eyes darted around as she reflected on the statement. "So, what was she expecting us to do? Turn her in or not turn her in? Is it a test?"

Kelly shrugged. "Maybe it's not even Kennedy. Everly seemed pretty convinced Melissa did it. Maybe these are from her!"

"Maybe. In which case, Kennedy wouldn't know anything about it."

"And maybe we're supposed to show it to her."

"Why give it to us? Why wouldn't Everly give it to her directly?"

"I don't know. I don't even know what we're supposed to do with this! Do we confront Melissa? Do we talk to Kennedy? Call the police?"

Jodi shrugged. "Has Kennedy called you back?"

Kelly checked her phone. "No. Nothing."

"Maybe we should go try to find her. At the very least, even if she does nothing with this information, I think someone should know we received it. It can be perceived as a threat."

"To us or Melissa?"

"Both!"

Kelly let her arms slap her sides. "Okay, I guess we'll go roaming around again in search of someone, anyone."

Kelly shoved the papers back into the envelope with a sigh.

They headed out the door again. "I wish we could lock the door behind us," Jodi said.

"Too bad we don't have a key," Kelly agreed.

After another trek down the monster staircase, they meandered through the halls. The library, occupied by Penny and Emily when they'd left, was now empty. Kennedy was nowhere to be found downstairs. Kelly tried to call her again, but received her voicemail message. She hung up in frustration.

"Now what?" she asked as they stood in the foyer. "Do we go upstairs and start knocking on random doors?"

"It's getting close to lunchtime; someone has to be somewhere."

As if on cue, a maid scurried past with a tray in her hands, climbing the stairs without so much as a nod to them.

"Or they're all 'ordering' food," Kelly said, waving her hand at the girl as she disappeared upstairs.

"That's an idea, though!"

"Order lunch?" Kelly asked.

"No, ask one of the staff where Kennedy's room is," Jodi said.

"Ohhhh, right! Good idea!"

"Looks like some of them are in the kitchen. Let's head there."

Kelly nodded in agreement, and they charged down the hall to the dining room, pushing through the door they'd used to retrieve their snack the night before. They descended to the kitchen, finding staff bustling around to complete lunches for the guests.

The butler oversaw the preparation. Kelly approached him, gently touching his elbow.

"Excuse me."

"Yes? Lunches will be up as soon as they are ready."

"Oh, okay, thanks. I have another question though."

"Oh, yes, of course. What is it?"

"Could you tell me what room Kennedy Moore is in?"

"Ms. Moore? I believe she is in the west hall, second door on the right as you enter."

Kelly smiled and nodded. "Thank you."

She retreated to where Jodi stood near the stairs. "Did you find out?"

Kelly nodded as they ducked into the stairway and headed up to the dining room.

"Where is she?" Jodi asked.

"West hall, second door on the right."

"Where's the west hall?"

Kelly shrugged. "I don't know. I didn't want to ask and sound like an idiot."

"But now we still have no idea where to go!"

"How hard can it be?" Kelly questioned, as they strode down the hall to the foyer. "We just figure out which way is west and then go to that hall."

"Oh, okay, perfect. Which way is west?"

"How should I know?"

"Exactly."

They climbed to the top of the stairs as Kelly fiddled with her phone. "Okay, I installed a compass app. West is... this way." Kelly stared at her phone and then pointed. She took two steps before she stopped. She spun in the opposite direction. "No, this way."

Jodi rolled her eyes. "Are you sure?"

"Yes," Kelly said with a sigh. "Sort of."

They stalked down the hall, approaching the second door on the right. Kelly shot a glance at Jodi as they stared at the door. With a gulp, Kelly knocked at the door. No one answered.

"Try again. Louder this time."

Kelly held back rolling her eyes as she pounded on the wood again. After a moment, she pressed her ear against the door. "Kennedy!" she called.

With a shrug, she flung her arms out. "I guess she's not here."

"Or we went to the wrong hall."

"Do you want to find west, Jodi?" Kelly said with a huff.

"No," she admitted.

Kelly sighed. "I need to sit down and regroup. We need to think about what to do next."

"Okay, we'll head back to the bedroom."

They wound through the halls to their room. Jodi pushed in through the door, stopping short of entering.

"Jodi!" Kelly said, as she ran into her. "You need to call your stops!"

Jodi's jaw hung open and she stood speechless. Kelly glanced around her, searching for the reason for her sudden shock. Her expression matched Jodi's as she scanned the inside of the room.

Jodi's suitcase lay open and upside down on the floor. Most of the contents were sprawled across the hardwood. The bed had been ripped apart, and drawers were pulled out and toppled onto the floor.

"We were robbed!" Kelly shouted.

"I'm not sure robbed is the right word. Doesn't look like they took anything. They just scattered my stuff everywhere."

Kelly pushed past her sister, skirting the disaster area, and running through the bathroom. "Ugh! They hit my room, too!"

"Seriously?" Jodi asked.

Kelly returned to Jodi's room, leaning on the door jamb leading to the bathroom. "Yes, seriously."

"Why?" Jodi asked, as she snatched a few articles of clothing from the floor.

Kelly shrugged. "Were they looking for something?"

Jodi folded up her blouse before tossing it on the bed and righting her suitcase. "What?"

With a sigh, Kelly shook her head. "Proof of my guilt?"

"Well, they wouldn't have found that. And what would that even look like anyway? A hand-written confession?"

Kelly shook her head again as Jodi continued her clean-up effort. She bit her lower lip as she scanned the mess.

"You could help," Jodi said.

Kelly rolled her eyes but pitched in, setting down the incriminating envelope and fixing the fitted sheet on the mattress before tugging the flat sheet back into place.

"This is insane," Jodi said, scooping a boot from the floor. "What would they possibly hope to gain from this?"

"Really." Kelly straightened the brocade comforter. "It's not like they'd find the murder weapon here or something." She chuckled at her own statement before turning serious. "Wait a minute."

Kelly's eyes grew wide, and she dropped the corner of the comforter before racing back through the bathroom and into her bedroom. She scanned the items on the floor, finding a pile of her pearl paraphernalia. After dropping to her knees, she sorted through it.

"Come on, come on." After a moment, she sat back on her haunches. "Oh, no."

Jodi joined her. "What is it?"

"My second knife is gone."

CHAPTER 14

*J*odi's forehead wrinkled. "Who would break in and steal your knife?"

"Uh, someone looking to frame me for murder?" Kelly said.

"By doing what? Stealing your knife and stabbing Pearl again?"

"Maybe they're going to transfer my fingerprints onto the murder weapon."

Jodi paused, her face a mask of surprise. "First, I'm not certain that happens in real life. And second, the murder weapon probably already has your fingerprints on it from the shucking you did before dinner."

"So, then why did someone wreck our rooms and steal my knife?"

"I have no idea, but this is getting out of hand. First, the information accusing Melissa, and now this?"

Kelly shook her head and snatched the envelope containing the damning texts and will and stormed toward the door.

"Where are you going?" Jodi asked.

"To find someone to sort this out!" Kelly hollered over her shoulder.

Jodi scrambled to her feet and followed Kelly as she thundered down the hall. "Who?" she shouted after her.

"Whoever I come across first," Kelly answered, a determined look on her face. They roamed through the upstairs halls, but ran into no one.

Wandering around another corner, they came upon a single set of double doors. Kelly studied them. "Do you think this is anything?"

"How should I know?" Jodi asked.

"We came across this yesterday. Maybe it was Pearl's room."

"Maybe. It's the only room in this hall. Maybe she has an entire apartment or something."

"Maybe we'll find something in there," Kelly said, starting toward the door.

Jodi grabbed her arm and pulled her back. "Wait a minute. We can't just barge in there and start pawing through her stuff."

"Why not? Someone did that to us, *and* stole my knife."

"We'll really look guilty if we get caught."

"We look guilty anyway."

Kelly shook off Jodi's grip on her forearm and trudged down the hall. She wrapped her fingers around the doorknob, but before she could turn it, a shout startled her.

"Just what do you two think you're doing? Haven't done enough damage?"

Kelly spun to face their accuser. "Aurora," she said, as she recognized the redheaded woman storming toward her.

"Get away from that door!"

"Why? We want some answers here. Our room was–"

"I don't care what you want. You've caused enough trouble already. Leave poor Melissa alone."

Kelly crinkled her brow. "Melissa? We weren't–"

"Right, sure. You were just about to burst into Melissa's room, but I'm sure you weren't going to do anything to her, right?"

"Melissa's room?" Kelly questioned. "I thought–"

"Just stop," Aurora interrupted. "Get out of here. Leave Melissa alone. She doesn't need you badgering her after her mother's murder. Especially you two who are going to rob her blind!"

"We're not robbing her."

"Do you not know the meaning of stop? Go away and leave Melissa alone."

Aurora pushed past Kelly and stood in front of the doors, crossing her arms over her chest and raising her eyebrows.

Kelly opened her mouth to speak but shook her head, deciding it was a losing battle. "Fine," she said, as she stalked back down the hall toward a waiting Jodi.

"Good going," Jodi whispered, as they scurried down the hall and around the corner.

"How was I supposed to know that was Melissa's room?"

"Well, maybe that's why you shouldn't–" The balance of Jodi's statement was cut off by a blood-curdling scream.

Both women froze, their eyes going wide. Kelly's heart pounded at the sound. She spun to face the direction they'd come. "That sounded like it came from back there, didn't it?" she whispered.

Jodi shrugged. "Maybe."

Kelly rounded the corner. The double doors to Melissa's room stood open. "Help!" Aurora shouted from inside.

"Come on!" Kelly said to Jodi. They hurried down the hall to the bedroom suite. Kelly reached the doorway first and stopped as she took a step inside. Her mouth dropped open. "Oh my goodness!"

Jodi caught up, nearly toppling into Kelly as she ground to a halt at the scene.

Inside, Aurora stood at the foot of the bed with her hands clasped over her mouth and her eyes wide with shock. She stared ahead at Melissa's form, laying in the bed. From Melissa's chest stuck Kelly's second shucking knife.

Aurora spun to face them, her face a mask of terror. "Get away from me!" she shouted.

"What?" Kelly questioned. "We need to get help!"

"Help for what? To kill me next? She's dead. Melissa is dead! And YOU killed her." Aurora poked her finger toward Kelly.

"No, I didn't!" Kelly shouted in her own defense.

Footsteps sounded in the hall behind them. Abby, Harper, and Everly appeared. The scene rendered them speechless. Tears fell onto Abby's cheeks. A few moments later, Reagan and Penny arrived.

"What's going on in here?" Reagan questioned.

Aurora sobbed. "She killed someone else! How long until we're all victims?"

"Oh, that's ridiculous," Kelly said. "I did not."

Harper spun to face her. "It's your knife! Again! Coincidence? I don't think so."

Aurora added, "And I just saw the two of them hovering at Melissa's door before I came in and found her."

"Yes, it's my knife. Someone stole it from my room. Our rooms were trashed and that was missing."

"I'll bet," Harper said. "A likely story."

"It's true!" Kelly exclaimed, heat entering her voice.

"Oh, how convenient," Everly chimed in. "I bet those two tossed their own room to make it look good."

"We did not!" Jodi shouted.

"This is insane," Kelly said. "Why would we kill Melissa? Or Pearl for that matter?"

"To make sure you get the money!" Harper shouted. "You knew Melissa would challenge the will. And you made sure she couldn't."

"That's a lie."

"I'll bet this knife has your fingerprints all over it."

"I'm sure it does. I picked it up a dozen times. It's *mine*. But I didn't do it."

"Yeah, right," Harper retorted. "First Pearl to get her money, and now Melissa to make sure you keep it."

"No!" Kelly insisted.

Reagan spoke up. "Ladies, we all need to calm down."

"I'm not going to calm down when there are two murderers standing mere feet away from me!" Aurora shouted.

"We should lock them up before they do any more damage!" Harper agreed.

"This is crazy! We didn't kill anyone!" Kelly shouted.

"I agree. Where can we put them?" Everly asked.

"This is insane," Jodi said.

Peyton and Aubrey entered the room, gasping at the sight.

"Reagan, do you know where there's a secure location to put these two?" Harper inquired.

"We could lock them in the pantry!"

"Are you insane?" Kelly asked. "First of all, I for one would like access to a bathroom and a chair."

"Kelly's right," Reagan said.

"Thank you."

"We should lock them in their bedrooms. We can barricade the doors."

"What? No, that's not what I meant."

"How can we barricade the doors?"

"A chair?"

"That's never going to work. We need to lock them up where they can't get away!"

"We could watch them. Take turns."

Kelly leaned toward Jodi. "Let's make a run for it. We'll lock ourselves in the bedroom as soon as we get there."

Jodi nodded. They slowly backed through the door. When they cleared it, Kelly spun on her heel and dashed down the hall. Jodi trailed behind her, her kitten-heeled boots making running harder.

"Hurry!" Kelly shouted, as she rounded the corner.

Shrieks sounded behind them as the women reacted to their flight. "They're getting away! Someone get them!"

They hurried through the halls. Pounding footsteps sounded behind them. Kelly gasped for breath as she rounded the final corner into their hallway. She streaked down the hall and into Jodi's room. With her head poking out the door, she encouraged Jodi to sprint the last leg.

"Hurry!"

Jodi ground to a halt.

"Jodi! Run!"

Jodi stared straight ahead. Kelly swung her head in the opposite direction. Harper approached from the opposite end. Kelly winced as Aurora rounded the other corner, closing the distance between her and Jodi.

With her jaw tensed, Kelly glanced inside the room. She grabbed the small round table from next to the armchair.

Kelly stepped to the door and flung the table at Harper, narrowly missing her.

Jodi hurried the final few steps and ducked into the room behind Kelly. Kelly stepped back and flung the door shut. It popped open as Aurora's hand reached inside.

"Help!" Kelly shouted to a winded Jodi. Together they pushed the door, trapping Aurora's hand inside. She yelped in pain before withdrawing her fingers. Kelly turned the lock, before collapsing against the door and breathing out a long breath.

Jodi panted for breath as they heard Aurora curse on the other side. She hurried around Kelly and circled a dresser, shoving at it from one side. "Help me!"

Kelly joined her and they pushed the dresser in front of their door.

"She may have broken my hand!"

"More collateral damage. They don't care! They're murderers!"

"We need to make sure they stay locked in there."

"Watch the door. I'll find something to tie the doorknobs together."

Kelly rolled her eyes at the statement before stalking to the bed and flopping onto it.

"This is insane. These people are crazy."

"One of them is crazy enough to be a murderer."

"But which one? We need to find out before someone murders us."

"Or locks us in a dungeon."

CHAPTER 15

Kelly sat up and opened the envelope she carried. She pulled the papers from within and tossed the container aside. With the documents spread across the bed, she studied them.

"What are you looking for?"

"Anything. Some clue. This was sent to us to make Melissa look guilty. Clearly, she's not. I doubt she killed Pearl then stabbed herself."

"Maybe she killed Pearl, and then someone killed her because of it?"

"Maybe, but I'd doubt it."

"Why?"

"Well, the murders were pretty similar. Which suggests the same person did it."

Jodi shrugged. "I guess it's probably pretty likely it was the same killer."

"And it wasn't me."

"Anybody had access to our room. It could be anyone."

Kelly reached over for her list. She crossed Melissa from

the top of the list. "Clearly, she's not guilty. At least, not of her own murder."

"Nope, down to fifteen suspects."

Kelly scanned the list. "Okay, let's compare these names to the names in the will."

She grabbed the bags of pretzels and popcorn. "Good thing we brought snacks last night. I don't think we'll be getting lunch."

Jodi dug into the pretzel bag. "We'll be lucky to be let out of our rooms, period."

Kelly bit into a pretzel as she flipped through pages. "Okay, it looks like no one really got much of anything, outside of Melissa."

"Do you think anyone knew that? What happens now, with Melissa dead?"

Kelly shrugged. "I'm not sure. I wonder if Melissa had a will?"

"She did!" Jodi announced.

"How do you know?" Kelly grabbed a handful of cheesy popcorn and tossed a piece in her mouth.

"I saw it in those file cabinets we went through. There was a folder called 'Melissa's Will'."

"Really? Why didn't you say anything?"

"Because we were looking for Pearl's will, not Melissa's."

Kelly rolled her eyes. "We could have used it right now."

"Well, sorry, I didn't realize Melissa would be murdered, too, and we'd need it!"

Kelly shook her head as Jodi threw a piece of popcorn at her, before grabbing another handful.

With a sigh, Kelly scanned her list again. "Okay, maybe later we can sneak out and get it. But for now, we need to make some kind of headway on this list."

"And money has been removed as a motive, because as far as anyone knows, we are inheriting the estate."

"But no one thinks that's going to stick, especially with my murder charge looming. So, this could still be about the money. Who would inherit from Melissa?"

"Wait!" Jodi exclaimed, as she glanced through the will.

"What?"

"There's a clause here that discusses what to do in case Pearl survives Melissa."

"But that doesn't matter," Kelly said. "Melissa did survive Pearl. Not for long, but she did."

"Yes, but it might tell us who may have had some motive of inheriting."

Kelly leaned over Jodi's shoulder as they waded through the legalese. "Here," Jodi said, pointing to a line. "In the event that I survive my daughter, Melissa Barlow, all items listed in clauses C through G, shall be passed on to my nieces equally. Then there's a list of them. Penelope, Addison, Parker."

Kelly put stars by their names on her list. "Okay, Penelope, Addison, and Parker stood to inherit if Melissa was out of the way. But only if Melissa was out of the way first."

Jodi flipped the page over and back several times. "What are you doing?" Kelly asked.

"Where's Willow?"

Kelly returned her gaze to her list, munching on another piece of popcorn. "How should I know? She's probably hiding out in her room."

"No, in the will."

"Why would she be in the will?"

"She's a niece. But her name is missing from the list."

Kelly grabbed the paper. "Let me see."

She read through the clause. "Maybe she was named somewhere else."

They spent thirty minutes poring over the legal document, but found no mention of Willow.

"Okay, she was left out entirely. I wonder why?" Jodi asked.

"Penny accused her of murdering Pearl. I wonder if she did it because she was left out of the will."

"That's pretty extreme," Jodi said.

"But it makes sense. She's been left out of the will. So you kill the woman who did it. And then you kill the person who stands to inherit everything."

"So this is more of a revenge killing than money-motivated?"

"Nothing else makes sense. I mean, it did when Melissa was our primary suspect, but not anymore. No one stood to inherit. Six months ago, Melissa thought she would inherit. Do you think everyone else knew that?"

"It stands to reason. But they know that's not true now, so why kill Melissa?"

"In the event that the current will reverts to this one if challenged."

"So, money could still be a motivator."

"Which puts Penelope, Addison, and Parker at the top of the list."

"Assuming the motivator was money. If it was revenge, maybe it's Willow for being left off the list."

Kelly glanced down at the page. After a moment, she circled Penelope multiple times.

"Got a theory?" Jodi asked.

"Penelope's name is on the list. Assuming this is money-motivated, and they thought the current will would be over-turned, Penelope stands to gain."

Jodi crunched on a pretzel. "So do Addison and Parker."

"But Penelope made sure to give us another suspect."

"Her mother didn't seem too happy about her airing dirty laundry."

"Didn't she? Or was that part of the plan?"

"So, what are you suggesting?"

"I'm suggesting out of the three of them, Penelope tried to shift the blame onto Willow. Maybe to deflect it from herself."

"What if she was telling the truth. Maybe Willow did kill them because she was left out of the will."

"What did Penelope say was her motive?"

"Something about Pearl killed her mother."

"Wait, what? That can't be right. Pearl killed her mother?"

"That's what Penelope said."

"No, she said…" Kelly waved her hand in the air. "Wait, it'll come to me." She paused, pressing her fingers into her forehead. "Pearl was responsible for her mother's death! That's it!"

"Okay, Pearl was responsible, Pearl killed her – same difference."

Kelly grabbed her phone and tapped on it. "Not really. 'Killed her' is like Pearl shot her or ran her over or something. 'Responsible for' is like Pearl was driving drunk and they were in an accident."

"Did you find anything?" Jodi questioned, leaning over Kelly's shoulder.

"So far, no. I don't know her name."

"Try 'Pearl Willow Barlow sister' in the search bar."

Kelly typed in the suggested search. "There're tons of articles here. Some of them are about Julia."

"Add obituary."

"Right." Kelly added the extra word to the search. "Bingo!" Kelly clicked on the article.

Jodi leaned further over her sister's shoulder as she scrolled through the long obituary. "Uh," she murmured. "Not much here. Just basic information. Who she is survived by and so on."

"Doesn't say how she died?"

"No, just says unexpectedly passed."

"Are there any other articles about her death? Try searching her name."

"Okay. She was Ruby Willow Garner."

"Wonder what happened with Julia?"

"What do you mean?" Kelly asked, as she typed in the name in the search bar.

"Pearl, Ruby, Julia. Did they run out of gemstones or what?"

"Guess they didn't want to continue the trend." Kelly clicked on an article titled *Willow Tragedy Leaves Family Grieving.* "Okay, let's see what this one says."

Kelly scanned the news article detailing Ruby's death. Jodi's eyebrows raised as she spotted the cause of death. She flicked her gaze to Kelly. Kelly's eyes met hers. "This says she committed suicide!"

Jodi screwed up her face. "How does that fall on Pearl?"

Kelly shrugged. "I don't know." She put a question mark next to Willow's name and jotted a note about her mother's death.

After another long look at the list, Kelly tossed it aside and stood. She paced around the room. "So, we have some more prominent suspects emerging on the list, but nothing solid."

"This is impossible. We really need more information."

"I wonder if Willow would be willing to talk to us."

"Even if she was, how would we get to her? And what would we ask? Hey, did you happen to kill Pearl and Melissa because Pearl somehow was responsible for your mother's suicide?"

Kelly paced around for a few more minutes before Jodi pulled the list over and studied it. "What about the friends?"

"Melissa's friends killed her?"

"Maybe one of them killed Pearl, and then Melissa turned

on them. Threw them under the bus. They slip us the evidence against Melissa."

"And then kill her so we know she didn't do it?"

Jodi tossed the list aside. "I don't know."

Kelly raked her fingers through her hair and blew out a long breath. "Me either. And I have a sinking feeling I'm going to be arrested whenever the police do get here."

"I don't know what we can do," Jodi said, with a sigh.

"Nothing. There's nothing we can do. Especially now! We're stuck in this stupid room."

"Maybe they left, and we can get out?"

"And do what?"

"I don't know! Wander around and get more evidence? Talk to the people who don't want to lock us in a dungeon?"

Kelly wandered to the door and wedged the dresser back enough to slide between it and the door. She eased the lock back, wincing as it clicked. She inched the door back. It barely opened, a rope holding it tight to the other outside. She managed to wrangle it open enough to peer through the crack. Harper paced the hall. Kelly guided the door closed as noiselessly as possible, quickly turning the lock.

"Nope. Harper the Fierce is out there patrolling the hallway. And they've got the doors tied together with rope."

"What about your doors?"

Kelly pointed a finger in the air. "I'll check."

She hurried from the room through the bathroom and eased her lock back. One tug told her these doors, too, were tied with rope. With a shake of her head, she clicked the lock back in place. She shuffled back into Jodi's room, shaking her head.

Jodi slumped her shoulders, flinging herself back into the pillows. "Stuck."

Kelly resumed her marching around the room. After

twenty minutes of nervous pacing, she settled on staring at the details on the walls.

"Could you imagine how much it would take to carve all these details?" Her fingers caressed a wooden rose in the corner of the room.

"They don't build 'em like they used to," Jodi agreed.

Kelly studied the detail on a golden sconce before moving on to a painting hanging on the wall. She crossed her arms and stared at it. "Who do you think this was? An ancient Willow?"

Jodi shrugged, still flopped back in the pillows, and staring at the ceiling. "Is there a name tag on it?"

"No," Kelly reported. She cocked her head. "It's crooked though. Someone must have messed it up when they dusted it."

She reached out to touch the intricately carved wooden frame. With her thumb and forefinger wrapped around the corner, she inched it back to being straight. It stuck for a second before it snapped into place. A loud bang sounded.

"What'd you do?" Jodi asked, pulling herself up to sit.

"Nothing!" Kelly's brow crinkled as she stared at the painting. A breeze wafted across her skin. She glanced in the direction as she touched her cheek. Her jaw dropped open and she spun to face Jodi. "Look!"

In the corner, the wall had fallen away, and a dark gaping hole stood in its place. Jodi raised her eyebrows as she slid off the bed. She crept across the room, staring into the darkness.

CHAPTER 16

"We're free!" Kelly squealed, as she stared at the secret passage opening.

"I wonder where this leads?" Jodi questioned.

"Let's find out." Kelly pulled her cell phone from her pocket and toggled on her flashlight.

"Wait!" Jodi said, grabbing Kelly's arm and stopping her.

"What?"

"Maybe we shouldn't go in there?"

"Why?"

"What if there's a trap in there? What if we get lost or stuck?"

"We can just backtrack and come here."

"What if we can't find our way back?"

Kelly hurried across the room and grabbed the bag of popcorn. "We'll leave a trail of popcorn." She waved the bag.

Jodi considered it. "Okay. Let me grab my phone in case your battery dies."

She crossed the room and swiped her phone from the night table.

"This is so exciting," Kelly said, as she crept into the dark-ened passage.

"If we actually inherited this house, we'd have a house with a secret passage."

"Yeah, and we could spy on the people we put in your bedroom."

"Ew, that's kinda creepy."

"But it could be fun," Kelly answered. They inched down the passage as darkness closed in around them. Kelly's cell phone shined its meager light ahead, but illuminated little. Jodi ran her hand along the wood beams creating the walls.

"I wonder where this is leading? Oh, give me the popcorn. I'll throw some down."

"Wait," Kelly said, pulling the bag closer to her. "This is a straight shot so far. Don't throw any."

"Why?"

"Because if we *do* inherit the house, I don't want a trail of popcorn in the walls, and then rodents."

"Ewww," Jodi squealed.

"Yeah. And I'm not dealing with mice or rats or whatever."

"You don't even deal with bugs."

"Nope. That's your job. Speaking of," Kelly said, shining her light into the crevices, "I hope there are no bugs creeping around in here."

"I'm sure there are."

Kelly winced. "Come on," Jodi answered. "It's our only way out."

The passage veered in another direction.

Jodi snatched the popcorn bag from Kelly's hand and pulled it open. "I really think we should throw down the popcorn."

"It's still straight."

"It turned!"

"But there was no fork or anything. So we wouldn't have to decide which way to go or anything. We just have to literally follow the path."

"Fine." Jodi crunched up the bag. "But if we come to a fork, I'm laying popcorn down, rats or not."

"Shhh," Kelly said.

"Don't shh me. I'm doing it. I don't want to be lost in here, roaming for days– "

Kelly waved her hand in the air before clamping it over Jodi's mouth. "Listen," she whispered.

Voices wafted through the air. Kelly lifted her hand. "Where's it coming from?" Jodi breathed.

Kelly crept down the hall further. She stopped as the voices became clearer, and pointed her finger toward one of the walls.

"Who is it?" Jodi inquired.

"How would I know?"

The voices continued to reverberate through the walls, sounding muffled. Kelly lowered her light as she pressed her ear against the wood. Jodi toggled on her own flashlight and shined it at eye level. Her eyebrows raised and she inched a wooden panel sideways. A sliver of light streamed from the room on the other side of the wall.

"Look!" she hissed. "A spy panel!"

Kelly jockeyed to reach the panel first and peer through.

"Hey! I found it. I should look first."

"Fine, go ahead, you baby."

Jodi peered through the sliver of an opening. "Who's in there?" Kelly whispered.

"Parker and Penelope," Jodi reported.

"Let me see," Kelly said, poking at Jodi.

"You're such a child. Go ahead."

Kelly peered into the room through the thin opening. A large bedroom lay on the other side. Parker sat in a wingback chair, her legs crossed. She sipped at a beverage as Penelope paced the room.

"I still can't believe this."

"Sit down, Penny, you'll wear a hole into the floor."

Jodi bumped Kelly with her hip. "Move over, there's room for both of us."

"Who cares? It's not our house anymore," Penelope answered.

"Do you really think those two hooligans are going to inherit?"

"Hey!" Kelly breathed. "Who's she calling a hooligan?"

Penelope nodded. "I think they stand a better chance with Melissa dead than they did with her alive. Will a judge really side with extended family? And wouldn't it go by Melissa's will at this point anyway? Who's will do we challenge?"

"Who is Melissa's heir?" Parker asked.

"I have no idea."

"What a mess this is. I'm afraid those two pearl sisters will steal the inheritance right out from under us with all the confusion."

"Not likely with the fleet of lawyers they'll be up against."

"Pearl's will was clear. I mean for Melissa's will to even apply, we'd have to get Pearl's current will thrown out."

"And with Melissa out of the picture, the biggest advocate for the will to be reversed is gone."

Parker shook her head. "I cannot believe they offed her. Probably for that reason."

"I'm not convinced they did it."

"Come on, who else would have done it?"

"Think about it, Parker," Penelope said, "why would they have killed Pearl? They couldn't possibly have known how much they'd stand to gain by her death."

"Maybe they did. Maybe they overheard the details being discussed at a lunch or–"

"Or where? In Pearl's private limo? In Kennedy's office?"

"Either. Maybe one of them is a secretary at the firm. Maybe a legal clerk. They could have gotten hold of the papers."

"And then roped Melissa into having a pearl party so they could kill Pearl?"

"It's plausible."

"It's a stretch," Penelope said.

"So, what's your idea then? Who would kill Pearl and Melissa?"

"Willow," she said matter-of-factly.

"Really?"

"Come on. She was the only niece not named in Pearl's will, and Pearl's responsible for her mother's suicide. She hates this family."

"Yet she's here every time there's an event. Like she's trying to get back into the will."

"Someone killed them. Who else would it be? Putting aside the pearl girls."

"I don't know. I cannot wait for this weekend to end."

Penelope sank into a chair next to Parker with a sigh and a murmur of agreement. Kelly motioned for them to continue down the hall.

Jodi closed the peephole and they snuck down the passage, rounding a corner before Kelly spoke, keeping her voice low.

"That's the second time Penelope mentioned Willow."

"Yeah, but Parker didn't agree."

"Maybe Parker did it."

"But why? She's the one who said it wouldn't help them unless the current will is thrown out. And it would mean they have a path to inherit through Melissa's will."

"We need to get Melissa's will," Kelly said.

"With any luck, this will lead us somewhere where we can make a run for it."

"Ugh, no more running, please. That last race from Melissa's room did me in. I think I pulled all my muscles."

"I wonder if there are any other peepholes."

Kelly stopped walking. "I'm not sure. We should check."

"Should we go back?"

Kelly continued forward. "No, maybe we should check on the way back. We also need to grab Melissa's will. And in order to do that, we need to find out where this ends."

"And if we can make it to and from the office from wherever this comes out."

"That's our priority."

"But if we happen past any other voices–"

"We'll look for a peephole. This could be a great way to get information."

They continued down the passage, which wound around several times before they arrived at an intersection.

"Should we go straight or right?" Kelly asked, flicking her flashlight's beam down each passage.

"Ummm…." Jodi hesitated as she snapped her gaze back and forth between them. "Straight."

"Are you sure?"

"No! Sure of what? I have no idea where these go!"

"Okay, we'll go straight."

"Should I put down some popcorn?"

"No, this is pretty obvious, I think."

"If we end up lost—"

"You'll be glad we didn't waste the popcorn."

They proceeded down the passageway, coming to a dead-end several feet down the passage. After a quick search, they found a peephole. The slit showed a large sitting room. Pictures of family littered the mantle above a large fireplace.

"This room looks like it's been lived in," Kelly said.

"Yeah. I wonder if it was Pearl's room."

"Maybe. Do you think we can get in there?"

"Let's look for a handle," Jodi suggested. Kelly shined her beam along the walls. In short order, they found a handhold. Jodi wrapped her fingers around it and pushed. "Nope."

"Try pulling."

Jodi tugged on the panel, and it gave way, revealing an entrance into the room. Kelly doused her flashlight as they stepped into the space, and shoved her phone into her pocket.

They spread out and studied the room. Kelly focused on the pictures scattered across the mantle. "These are all of Pearl with various people."

"I bet this was her suite."

"Yeah, that's what I'm guessing, too."

Kelly wandered to an archway leading to another room. A plump four-poster bed stood against the far wall. Across the room, a wooden vanity with a backless chair sat centered on the wall, wedged between two dressers. Kelly approached the table, eyeing the silver comb, brush, and mirror set. She spritzed perfume from the atomizer, sniffing at the rose-scented liquid as it disappeared in the air.

She wandered to the dresser and peeked in the top drawer.

"Seriously?" Jodi questioned from the door.

Kelly shrugged and slid the drawer shut. "Maybe she hid something in her underwear drawer."

"Like what? A note that says, 'here's who I think is going to kill me'?"

Kelly shrugged again and stalked over to the bed. She pulled open the drawer of the nightstand. It contained a pair of glasses, rosary beads, and a few loose throat lozenges. A book was shoved in the back of the drawer.

Kelly wiggled it free from the drawer and glanced at the

cover. "*Ghosts, Lore and a House by the Shore,*" she read from the cover, before flipping it over. "Hmm, she must have liked cozy mysteries."

Kelly flipped open the front cover. Several papers fluttered to the floor below as she perused the first chapter.

Jodi scooped the papers off the floor and shuffled through them. "Oh my gosh!" she exclaimed.

"What is it?" Kelly asked, ceasing her reading for a moment.

"These notes… they're all threats!"

CHAPTER 17

Kelly studied Jodi, who clutched the notes in her hand, a stunned expression on her face.

"What? Does it say who they are from?"

Jodi shook her head and shared the papers with Kelly. *"You'd better think about what you're doing. I'm owed something, too,"* Kelly read aloud.

Jodi flipped to the next page and read, *"You're a thief, and you're going to pay for it one way or another."*

"Whoa!" Kelly exclaimed, as Jodi shuffled to the last paper. *"You can't ignore me. You'll regret it if you do."*

"Someone really hated Pearl," Jodi said.

"Yeah, but who?"

Jodi shrugged. "There's no name on these."

"Why didn't Pearl report this?"

"Maybe she did."

"And no one knows? Clearly this person was threatening her. They'd be the prime suspect in her murder! Did no one in her family know about this?"

Jodi flicked her gaze to Kelly. "Maybe they did."

Kelly's eyebrows raised high, and she offered Jodi a knowing expression.

"Willow," they both repeated at the same time.

"This points to her guilt, right?" Kelly said, glancing at the notes again.

"Maybe," Jodi hedged.

"Well, look." Kelly pointed to one note. "'I'm owed something, too'. She was left out of Pearl's original will. The one where Melissa inherits everything and if Melissa dies first, the nieces inherit."

"Yep," Jodi agreed. "It does fit with that."

"And then this one. 'You're a thief'. It could mean she's robbing her of her inheritance."

Jodi nodded in agreement. "And this last one," Jodi added, "'you can't ignore me, you'll regret it' definitely sounds like a threat."

"Like if you keep ignoring me, I'm going to kill you. And she may have given this to her when she arrived, then killed her when Pearl didn't bother to do anything about it!"

"We may be on to something here," Jodi said.

"We need to get Melissa's will and see if that gives us any clues."

"Maybe the other passage will lead to another spot where we can get closer."

"We have no idea where we are right now," Kelly said.

"Right, and I don't want to be roaming through the halls with the crazy people who are trying to lock us up for something Willow did!"

Kelly nodded and they retraced their steps to the secret passage. Jodi stepped inside but Kelly hesitated in the room. "What are you waiting for?" Jodi asked.

"Maybe we should try to find the trigger for this one."

Jodi considered it. "What if we can't find it?"

"You stay in there and I'll look for it."

Jodi wrinkled her nose. "Why do I have to stay in the creepy passage alone?"

"Because someone has to stay in there in case I can't find the trigger."

Jodi rolled her eyes. "Fine." She pushed the passage shut.

Kelly scanned the walls surrounding it. "Maybe it's the painting like it was in the last room!" she shouted. She grabbed the painting and slid it from side to side. The panel remained closed.

"Nope!" Kelly yelled. "Not the painting."

A muffled sound came from behind the wall.

"What?" Kelly hollered.

"I said try the sconce."

"Ohhh, right, the sconce." Kelly studied the brass object on the wall. She grabbed it and tugged it to each side. "Nope!"

Kelly pressed a few decorative items on the trim work.

"Did you pull the sconce?"

"Yeah, I pulled it left and right."

"Did you try down?"

Kelly wrinkled her nose. "Oh, yeah, down." She grabbed the sconce again and yanked it toward the floor. The passage slid open.

Jodi stood inside with her arms crossed. "Seriously? You didn't try down?"

"It didn't occur to me, okay? The painting went sideways."

Jodi rolled her eyes as Kelly stepped into the passage. "Anyway, at least now we know in case we need it."

"Or we inherit and one of us takes Pearl's bedroom."

Kelly flicked on her flashlight and led the way toward the intersecting passage. "I don't know if I want it. That's sort of creepy."

"Why? She didn't die in there?"

"No, I guess not. The living room might be haunted, though."

Jodi side-eyed Kelly. "So, you taking Pearl's old room, or what?"

"Like that's ever going to happen. We'll be in court from now until we die over this."

They reached the crossroads and hung a left into the unexplored passage. It veered around several corners before they came to a rickety wooden staircase. Kelly eyed it suspiciously. "This looks unsafe."

"Well, we're either going back to Pearl's and trying to find our way downstairs or we're trying these stairs."

"Okay, it may be safer to try these stairs since the worst that can happen is we fall, versus we're hunted down by Melissa's vicious friends and locked up."

"I'll go first since you're a wimp." Jodi placed her foot gingerly on the top step. She tested the pressure, transferring her weight bit by bit. After a moment, she brought her other foot down onto the step. She bounced around a bit. "Seems sturdy."

"I'll wait until you're down at the bottom."

"Suit yourself." Jodi toggled on her cell phone's flashlight and ambled down the steps, disappearing into the darkness below. Kelly only spotted the bobbling light at the bottom waving an all-clear.

She descended the stairs, hanging onto the walls in case the wood gave way. After making it safely to the bottom, she glanced around for Jodi, who was nowhere to be found.

"Jodi!" she whispered into the darkness.

A bobbling light turned toward her. "Here."

"What are you doing?"

"Looking for a peephole to see where we are."

"Oh, smart! Did you find one?"

"Not yet."

They continued down the passage, each keeping their flashlights on and searching the walls as they went. They stumbled upon one a few feet down the passage. It looked into one of the back sitting rooms, though the space was empty.

"No eavesdropping here," Kelly said.

"Nope. Do you think there's an opening into there?"

They spent a few minutes searching, not finding anything. "Guess there's no entry into that room."

"I hope there's a way out down here," Jodi said.

"Yeah, and it's close to the office with Melissa's will."

After another few moments of walking, they arrived at a dead end. "Let's hope there's an exit here, otherwise we're going to be backtracking and searching the walls," Jodi said.

She set the popcorn bag down and fumbled around until her fingers caught in a crevice and the wall inched back toward her.

"Success!" Kelly exclaimed.

"Yeah, but no peephole to see if anyone is there."

"We're going to have to fix that if we own this place," Kelly said, as she peered through the crack into the room beyond.

"Where are we?" Jodi whispered.

"The garden room. Looks empty."

Jodi pulled the panel back further and they scanned the space before stepping inside, hidden behind a tall bush.

"At least they hid the entrance behind something," Jodi said.

"Yeah. Wait, should we figure out how to open this?" Kelly asked.

"We'd better. We'll have to come back this way. This time you go in the scary secret passage and wait."

"Okay," Kelly said, ducking back inside the passage. She toggled on her flashlight as she pushed the panel closed, plunging the space into darkness. Within moments, a sliver of light filtered in, and Jodi pushed the panel open.

"How'd you get that so fast?"

"I'm smart," Jodi said.

"No, really, how'd you do it?"

"That's kind of rude. I can't believe you don't think I'm smart."

"I didn't say that. Come on, how did you figure it out?"

"There's not many options to try here. I figured it was this hanging flowerpot thing," Jodi said.

"Oh, right. Good, so we can come back this way."

"Yep," Jodi confirmed. "Now, let's see if we can get to the office and grab that will."

Kelly nodded in agreement, and they wound through the flowering bushes to the entrance. They backtracked through the empty hall toward the back of the house.

As they rounded the corner, voices wafted from one of the rooms down the hall. Kelly held up a finger, signaling to halt their progress. She motioned toward the room with the door partially ajar. Jodi nodded, and together they crept down the hall, approaching the open door.

They peered in through the opening. Reagan and Peyton stood inside.

"...should do?" Reagan asked.

"Nothing," Peyton answered, with a shrug.

Reagan's brow furrowed.

"Why would we do anything?" Peyton questioned. "I never agreed with the original will. I could care less if this one stands."

"So you're willing to let this all go outside of the family?"

Peyton crossed her arms. "It wasn't staying in *my* family anyway. And why do you care? Neither you nor your daughter was named. It all went to Melissa. And now that she's dead, we have no idea who it would go to if the will is reversed. Who was Melissa's heir?"

"I don't know. And like you said, it would only matter if we had the current will revoked and the old will put in place."

"And as I already stated, I have no desire to help do that. Pearl is a thief. I'd just as soon let the property go to a stranger off the street than back to the Willows only."

"That's a little harsh, Peyton. Do you really hate our family that much?"

"I hate the fact that the Willows were broke until Pearl married my cousin and he dumped all his money into their accounts to save this place. And now she's cut off the Barlows entirely. She took all that money, kept this house, and then promised it to Willows only."

"Not all the Willows. Plus, Melissa is a Barlow."

"No, she notoriously left Willow out of the mix, didn't she? First, she drives her mother to suicide, then she cuts her out of the will for being born to a weak-willed woman. Pearl was full of herself. And Melissa was even worse. Besides Melissa is dead, so she's not getting it, is she?"

"Penelope was named in the will, Emily."

"Only in the event Melissa was dead, and that was more about slapping Willow in the face than anything."

"I think it's a travesty if it goes to those two."

"I don't. Someone here murdered Pearl and Melissa. And it wasn't those dim-witted pearl slingers."

"Who's she calling dim-witted?" Jodi hissed.

Kelly waved her hand to signal her into silence.

"Then who?"

"Willow certainly had enough reason."

"So, you think Willow did it?"

Peyton shrugged. "I certainly couldn't blame her if she did

it. But Pearl made a lot of enemies. It could have been any one of them."

Reagan furrowed her brow. "Who else was her enemy here?"

Peyton smirked and waved her hand in the air. "Take your pick, Reagan, the house is full of people who hated Pearl for one reason or another this weekend."

Kelly shifted her weight to get a better look in the room. In the process, her hip nudged the door. A loud creak split the silence. Kelly winced as the door's groaning announced their presence.

Both women inside snapped their head in the direction of the slightly ajar doors.

Peyton narrowed her eyes at the entrance. "What was that?"

"I'm not sure."

Peyton stepped around Reagan and headed for the door.

"Run!" Kelly whispered.

CHAPTER 18

She and Jodi scrambled down the hall, ducking into another room and praying it was unoccupied. Footsteps stormed past their location. Jodi grasped the handle to pull open the door, but Kelly stopped her, holding her finger up in a silent gesture to wait.

Moments later, another pair of feet pounded past. They strained to listen as the footsteps disappeared down the hall and around the corner.

"Do you think it's safe?" Jodi whispered.

"I hope so. We need to get to that will."

"And then back to our room to discuss what we just heard!"

"Yeah!" Kelly said with a nod. "Okay, let's make a run for the office."

"No running, remember?"

"Okay, let's make a reasonably quick walk to the office."

Jodi agreed and they inched the door open, peering up and down the hall. Nothing. After ensuring it was clear, they ducked out of the door and hurried to the corner. Kelly and Jodi peered around it and found that hall empty, too.

They hurried halfway down to the office door and slipped inside. "Quick!" Kelly breathed. "Grab the will."

Jodi darted to the file cabinet she'd searched earlier and yanked open the drawer. Her face turned into a mask of confusion, and she flicked her gaze to Kelly. "It's not here!"

"What?" Kelly cried.

"It was right here in this drawer earlier! Now it's gone!"

"Oh, great! Are you serious? We did all this for nothing?"

Jodi stood. "Looks like it."

"Maybe it's somewhere else in here."

They spent a few moments searching the room, but found no traces of the will. As they dug through the desk drawers, the door to the room popped open. Kelly and Jodi ducked behind the desk as the strawberry-blonde strode into the room, closing the door behind her. She cocked her head, planting a hand on her hip.

"I can see you," she said.

Kelly and Jodi rose slowly, peering over the desk before they rose to stand. Kelly grabbed a paperweight, brandishing it in the air. "Don't come any closer," she warned.

"I'm not here to hurt you."

"No, just to lock us up!" Jodi shouted.

Abby shook her head. "No, I'm not part of that. I've been looking for you everywhere since the others said they locked you in your room, but you weren't answering them."

Kelly's brow furrowed and Abby continued. "They've been trying to yell through the door to you. I suggested you weren't going to answer them since they've been total jerks to you, but I wondered if you'd found a way out."

Kelly remained silent, unwilling to give away any information on how they achieved their escape.

Jodi crossed her arms over her chest and arched an eyebrow. "I don't believe you."

Abby shrugged. "You don't have to, but I'm one of the few allies you have."

"Why would you help us?"

"Simple. I don't believe you killed Pearl or Melissa. And I want justice for them both, especially Melissa."

Kelly narrowed her eyes at Abby.

"I'm being honest," Abby said. "There's no reason for you to have killed either Pearl or Melissa."

"Ugh, thank you!" Kelly exclaimed.

"It doesn't make any sense," Abby answered. "Someone is working hard to frame you."

"You must have some idea of who did it," Jodi said.

"No," Abby answered.

"Did Melissa say anything to you before she was murdered about who she thought did it?"

Abby shook her head. "She didn't even want to discuss it. I assumed it was the grief, but now I'm wondering if she was afraid of something or someone."

"What do you mean? Why would you think she was afraid?"

"Just the way she acted. There was no love lost between Melissa and her mother, so I thought it was odd when she acted the way she did. I assumed the murder was a shock, one she wasn't prepared for. But in retrospect, I'm wondering if she was shocked for a different reason."

"So, you think she knew who the murderer was and didn't say anything because she was afraid," Jodi said. "But afraid of what? Of being murdered?"

"Maybe that or maybe afraid of something else. Some family secret getting out? She mentioned something to me a few months ago about her family having more secrets than anyone knew."

"Do you have any idea who would profit from this? Assuming the Willows could get Pearl's original will reinstated, Melissa would inherit. And since Melissa is dead, it would be whoever she named who would profit. Do you know who she'd named?"

"No," Abby answered, "but I do know she made a recent change to her will. She didn't tell me what it was, but she did it right around the time she told me her family had secrets."

"Did she say why?" Jodi asked.

"She said she had to do it."

"Because of her mother or what?" Kelly inquired.

"No. She didn't blame it on Pearl. But it seemed to be related to whatever this family secret was. She wasn't happy about it, but she said she had to do it until she could figure out how to handle the situation. She said it was sensitive." Abby flung her arms out to the side. "That's all I know."

Jodi poked a finger at the drawer. "Someone removed the will from this drawer for a reason."

Abby nodded at her assessment. "I'd say so. Likely the guilty party."

"We need to find that will," Kelly said, wringing her hands.

"I'll work on finding a copy of the will. Maybe Kennedy has one," Abby said.

"We haven't been able to get a hold of her."

"She's been tied up with the police and dealing with Pearl's will. And now with Melissa dead, well, she has her hands full."

"I'll bet," Kelly said, flinging her hands out. "And our hands are tied. We can only sneak around because people are out for our blood."

"I know. They won't listen to reason."

"Do you think one of them is guilty?" Jodi asked.

"One of our group? Melissa's friends? I don't see why they would have done it. What would they stand to gain?"

"Maybe it was simple jealousy," Kelly suggested.

"Stranger things have happened, but this doesn't seem like jealousy. Someone had a plan. We just have to figure out who it was and what they were after."

"I agree. If you can get a hold of that will, we can see if it offers any clues," Jodi said.

"Okay, how are you leaving your room? So I can get back to you once I've tracked down information on my end."

"Uh-uh," Kelly said. "We are not telling you that."

Abby arched an eyebrow. "How do you propose we meet?"

Kelly held up her cell phone. "I'll give you my number. Text us when you have something, and we'll set up a place to meet."

"Okay," Abby agreed.

They exchanged numbers before they parted ways. Kelly and Jodi insisted Abby leave first. She obliged, disappearing down the hall with a flick of her strawberry blonde curls.

"Wow," Kelly said as they waited. "What was that about?"

"I'm not sure, but I'm glad she didn't turn us in."

"Me too. Maybe she can help."

"Let's get back to the bedroom where we can talk about what she told us and what we overheard between Reagan and Peyton."

"Okay, straight to the garden."

Jodi nodded and Kelly eased the door open, peeking up and down the hall. "Clear," Kelly whispered.

They slipped out the door, hurrying down the hall and around the corner. As they rounded the bend, Willow stood in the middle of the hall. Jodi and Kelly twisted away from her, hoping to escape, but she caught sight of them.

"I wouldn't do that if I was you."

Kelly winced as she turned back to face the woman.

"Hi, Willow," she said, forcing a smile onto her face.

"How'd you two escape protective custody?"

"Uh, it was less protective and more wrongful imprisonment," Jodi countered.

Willow chuckled at the statement. "Melissa's friends are idiots."

Kelly narrowed her eyes at the woman. "I guess they're concerned about having a killer running around," she said.

Willow shrugged. "It's obviously not you two. Why would you kill Melissa?"

"Why would they think we'd kill Pearl?"

"All they think of is money. Someone here probably killed for it. So, they think everyone will."

"But–"

"You couldn't know you were inheriting. That would be obvious if they took two seconds to think, instead of just freaking out that they weren't getting the money."

"Right! We had no idea!"

"Neither did they, and that's what gets their goat."

"So, it was really a surprise? No one knew Pearl had changed her will?"

"Nope," Willow answered. "Last we knew, Melissa got it all."

"And if Melissa was dead, then what?"

"The nieces inherited. Oh, all the nieces except yours truly." She waved her hand toward herself.

"Didn't that make you mad?" Kelly asked.

Willow rolled her eyes. "Seriously?"

"Well, being left out of the will while all your cousins are mentioned seems like a real slap in the face. No one could blame you. I'd be mad," Jodi said.

"I told you before. I don't want anything from Pearl Willow Barlow."

"Why?" Kelly inquired.

"My business, not yours."

"Oh, come on," Kelly coaxed. "You're left out of the will.

There's obviously some animosity between you and Pearl or the entire family."

"Maybe enough to warrant you to kill someone?" Jodi suggested.

"Seriously?" Willow said, with an unimpressed stare. "I could have screamed the second I saw you and had you locked up by Melissa's merry band of whack jobs, but I didn't. And all so you could accuse me of murder?"

"No one's accusing you of murder, Willow," Kelly assured her. "But after they finally realize it wasn't me, they're going to accuse someone, and you seem to be at the top of the list. Even we think you look guilty."

"Well, I'm not," she snapped.

"But you have every reason to hate Pearl. So, what happened between you? Why leave you out of the will?"

Willow grimaced and drew in a deep breath. "Pearl killed my mother."

"I thought your mother committed suicide?"

Willow's frown deepened. "Yes, thank you for bringing up one of the most painful memories of my life."

"I'm sorry, but everyone else keeps bringing it up. We've heard it at least three times being discussed amongst the family It's only a matter of time until they stop accusing us and start accusing you. They're already lining up to do it," Kelly said.

"And you never answered," Jodi said. "If your mother committed suicide, how did Pearl kill her?"

"Simple," Willow answered. "She badgered at her and badgered at her until she finally couldn't take anymore. She needled at my mother about being a failure, about how weak she was, and how any problems we had were her fault.

"My mother struggled with depression. And at one low point, Pearl stopped by our house. She spent over an hour basically torturing her with her comments. After Pearl left, my mother walked into her bathroom and slit her wrists.

"After that, Pearl disinherited me because I came from weak stock. She thought because she had all the money, it made her better than she was. That it gave her some kind of power over the rest of us. The real irony is it wasn't even her money."

"I'm really sorry, Willow," Kelly said.

"Me too. But the last thing I'd do is kill Pearl."

Kelly crinkled her brow at the statement. Willow shrugged. "It's too easy. I want her to have to live with what she did every day of her life. And I wanted her to have to live with the fact that her own daughter couldn't stand her. And that she had no real family. From the video we watched this morning, I'd say she understood that. It's just too bad she didn't have to live with it longer."

"Okay, say we buy your story. That you hated Pearl enough to kill her, but you didn't. Then who did?"

Willow shrugged again. "I don't know. I thought Melissa did it for the money. But she can't be the killer unless she did it, and then someone else killed her."

"We thought of that, but ruled it out. What're the chances they'd kill in the same way?"

"Could be a copycat."

"But why?" Jodi asked.

"To blame you. They're your knives."

"We lack motive. Especially when it comes to Melissa."

"You could make the case you killed Melissa to stop a legal challenge."

Kelly rolled her eyes.

"I didn't say I believed that. I just said you could make that case."

"Well, we didn't do it. So, who did?"

"I have no idea," Willow said. "I just can't wait to be out of this house." She took a few steps down the hall." But you may want to work faster to find out before they string you two up. At the very least, you may want to scurry back to your bedroom."

She began to circle around them, when she stopped and cocked her head, staring at Kelly's pocket. "Why do you have a picture of Everly in your pocket?"

Kelly glanced down at it. "Oh, I found it on the floor while we were exploring. I stuck it in my pocket and forgot about it."

"I would have left a picture of any of Melissa's despicable friends on the floor and kept on going." Willow continued down the hall. "Good luck!" she called behind her.

She disappeared around the corner and Kelly glanced at Jodi. "Well, that was weird."

"Par for the course in this house."

"So, Pearl badgered her mother literally to death."

"According to Willow," Jodi said.

"Yeah, but—"

Kelly's response was cut off by a shrill shriek. "You!" Aurora shouted. "How did you two get out?"

Kelly's eyes went wide, and her muscles tensed. "Run!" she shouted to Jodi, grasping her arm.

CHAPTER 19

"Help! Help! The murderers are loose! Help!" Aurora screamed.

Kelly tugged Jodi down the hall. Aurora raced after them, her four-inch heels slowing her pace enough to allow Kelly and Jodi to widen the gap between them.

They rounded the corner. Madison stood in the hall. She balled her hands into fists and narrowed her eyes. She kicked her shoes off and sprinted down the hall, pumping her arms like an Olympic runner.

"Hurry!" Kelly squealed, as they sprinted across the hall and ducked into the garden. Kelly slammed the doors behind them, and they wound through the rose bushes, ducking behind one. Jodi yanked the plant hanger down and the panel popped open.

The door swung open across the room as Kelly ducked into the passage. She waved Jodi inside and they pushed the panel closed. Kelly leaned against it, gulping in air.

"We know you're in here," Aurora shouted.

"You can't get away this time, killers!" Madison added.

In the dark, Kelly rolled her eyes and shook her head. "Are they serious?" she whispered.

Moments later, a new voice entered the mix. "What's going on?" Harper inquired.

"The killers escaped from their room! We chased them in here."

"Spread out and search for them. They can't have gone far," Harper said.

Kelly and Jodi waited a few moments as the women searched the garden.

"They're not here!" Madison shouted.

"They must have gone outside," Harper answered.

"In the rain?" Aurora questioned.

"We need to call the police. They're trying to get away," Harper said.

"I'll call 9-1-1 and tell them there are two murderers on the loose," Madison answered.

Kelly toggled on her flashlight. "I've heard enough, let's get out of here."

Jodi nodded and grabbed the bag of popcorn. It crinkled loudly. Jodi froze.

"What was that?" Aurora asked.

"Shh!" Kelly warned.

"I heard something. Something crinkling."

"Sorry!" Jodi hissed.

"If you're in here, we're going to find you!" Harper shouted.

"Let's go!" Kelly breathed.

Jodi nodded, causing the bag to crinkle again. Kelly slumped her shoulders and huffed as they hurried down the passage. They proceeded past the sitting room before they reached the rickety stairs. One after the other, they climbed up and wound through the halls and back to their bedroom.

Kelly blew out a sigh of relief as they stepped back into Jodi's bedroom. "You almost got us caught!"

"Sorry! But I didn't want to leave the popcorn behind. It might be the only food we get for the rest of the day."

"I hope they don't find the secret passage."

"They didn't seem to know about it."

Kelly plopped onto the bed. "What is going on here?"

"They're still foaming at the mouths to rip us to shreds."

"Not that. I mean who killed Pearl and Melissa?"

"Oh," Jodi said, crossing the room and flinging herself onto the other side of the bed. "That."

"Yeah, that," Kelly said. The reason we're hiding in our room and creeping around secret passages."

"I don't know."

"Willow insisted she didn't do it."

"Do you really think she'd admit to it if she did?"

Kelly considered it. "No."

"So, she's still our top suspect."

"Only because she hated Pearl. But did she hate Melissa?"

"Maybe. She seems to have hated the whole family."

"What if it was one of the Barlows? They seemed pretty mad about being cut out of the will," Jodi said, grabbing Kelly's suspect list.

Kelly glanced over her shoulder. "But why kill Pearl? It didn't help them; it just ensured no Barlow got their money."

Jodi scrunched her nose. "Okay, point taken. So, let's cross them off the list. They had no motive. They weren't in the will. And killing Pearl only made sure they'd never see the money."

"Wait," Kelly said, as Jodi retrieved a pen and held it over Emily's name.

"What?"

"What if it was a revenge thing?"

"We have to cross someone off," Jodi said.

Kelly nodded. "Okay. You're right, they probably didn't do it."

Jodi nodded and struck a line through Emily's name and Peyton's name. Her pen hovered over Penelope.

"Wait, keep her. She stood to gain in the original will."

"Right. But only if Melissa was dead. And she wasn't when they killed Pearl."

"Maybe Melissa's will named them, too. Maybe they needed both Pearl and Melissa dead."

"We need a copy of that will." Kelly checked her phone for a message from Abby. "Nothing from Abby yet."

"Can we get rid of the crazy friends?"

"Yes," Kelly said. "They have no motive, and they wouldn't have killed Pearl for Melissa, and then killed Melissa."

Jodi crossed off Abby, Harper, Aurora, Madison, and Everly. Kelly leapt to her feet and paced the floor.

"You don't think Abby did it and is covering it up by helping us?"

Jodi wrote Abby's name again above the crossed-off name.

"I didn't say she did, I just asked."

With puckered lips, Jodi crossed her off again.

"But do you think?"

Jodi's shoulders slumped and she huffed. "Will you stop flip-flopping around?"

"I can't help it! We can't solve this! We have too little information!"

"We have to rule some people out." Jodi tapped then against the paper. "What about Kennedy?"

"She's MIA. Could she have killed Pearl?"

"Why?"

"No reason, cross her off."

Jodi nodded and scratched her name off the list. "Julia."

"She seemed really upset and plus in the grand scheme of

things, I can't imagine she had the wherewithal to run across the room and stab Pearl."

Jodi crossed her off.

"If you disagree, please say something."

"I don't disagree. And we have to narrow it down somehow so we can try to find evidence or confront someone."

"Confront someone? I'm not confronting anyone!"

"How are we going to solve this then?"

"Well, not by confronting someone. I don't have a death wish. This person has killed two people!"

"Fine, fine, let's keep going. Are we keeping Willow?"

Kelly ceased her pacing for a moment as she considered it. "No. I believe her."

Jodi wiggled her eyebrows, but crossed her off.

Kelly cocked her head. "Do you disagree?"

"No, she seemed honest. And she's kind of obvious. Everyone suspects her, she'd never get away with it."

Kelly spun on her heel and stalked across the room in the other direction. "Who's left?"

"Penelope, Addison, and Parker. Reagan and Aubrey."

"Cross off Reagan and Aubrey. They had no motive. They're not in the will."

Jodi's pen slid across the paper, striking more people from the list. "Okay."

"And should we add back Emily and Peyton?"

"Why?"

"Peyton was mad the Barlows were cut off. Did she kill her out of anger?"

"And ensure the Barlows were cut off?"

"You're right. Leave them crossed off." Kelly collapsed onto the bed. "So, Penelope, Addison and Parker are our top suspects. But which one of them did it?"

"Penelope," Jodi suggested.

"Why?"

"She kills Pearl, then Melissa because —" Jodi paused. "No, never mind. They don't make sense either. They only stood to gain if Melissa died first."

"Unless they're named in Melissa's will."

"And if they are, my money's on Penelope, because by killing them she gets some of the Barlow money back."

"That's weak."

"So is accusing us, but that didn't stop anybody."

"But it's too weak to get the police to stop looking my way when the whole house accuses me except the black sheep, Willow."

"Speaking of Willow, Penelope is also the one who has been accusing Willow at every turn."

Kelly raised her eyebrows. "You're right!"

"And how better to get the attention off yourself than to accuse someone else?"

"Right!" Kelly agreed. "Oh, do you think Penelope is the culprit? Where was she during Pearl's murder?"

"She was right next to Pearl when she died! She's the one who said she was dead!" Jodi exclaimed.

Kelly's eyes widened. "She did it! It was Penelope!"

"I'll bet you anything she's in Melissa's will!"

"Yep. And I wonder if she stands to get a bigger share in Melissa's will."

"Either way, I'll bet she gets something with them both dead."

"If she can get the current will thrown out."

They were silent for a moment as they mulled over the information. Kelly bounced off the bed again and paced the floor. "We need to do something about this."

"What?"

"Tell someone."

"Who?" Jodi questioned.

"Kennedy, Willow, one of Melissa's mob – anyone who will listen! They have the wrong people locked up! Penelope is out there roaming free!"

"Do you think anyone will listen?"

"We have to *make* them listen," Kelly said. "If we don't say anything, we're going to be accused of a murder we didn't commit the second the cops get here."

"Okay, fine," Jodi said, climbing off the bed with a sigh. "I guess we'll go try to find someone and tell them we think Penelope did it."

Kelly pushed the painting to trigger the secret panel. It slid open, and they entered with Kelly's flashlight toggled on. Thunder rumbled overhead as they stepped inside.

"Why does it have to be storming when we have to do this?" Kelly lamented.

"It's been storming all weekend."

"I know! What a creepy place to be for a rainy weekend."

"Better get used to it. It'll be just as creepy when we move in here."

Kelly rolled her eyes. "I'll believe that when I see it."

"What are you going to do if we inherit this place?"

"Throw a party," Kelly said.

"Really? Like a huge pearl party?"

"Just a party. Are you kidding? Going from our two-bedroom to this?"

"We could sleep in a different bedroom every night and not make it through the entire house in a week."

"I know! Though actually, the first thing you were going to do is get me an elevator."

"I'll call the minute we sign the papers."

"Remember that," Kelly said.

They approached the peephole into the bedroom they'd spotted Penelope and Parker in earlier.

"Do you think anyone is in there?"

"Let's check." Jodi eased the sliding cover open and peered through the slit. Penelope paced the room alone.

"Look at her in there like a caged lion," Kelly said.

"Probably the guilt is eating her up," Jodi said.

"Yeah. She's wondering if she can get away with framing us for the murder." Kelly shook her head and narrowed her eyes at the woman.

A knock sounded at the door, and Penelope hurried across the room. She swung the door open to find her mother, Emily. Emily waltzed into the room with a tray. Two cups and a teapot sat on top.

"Thank God," Penelope said, collapsing into the chair. "My nerves are shot."

"Calm down, Penny," Emily said, as she poured the tea.

"How can I? Is there any word from the police?"

"They won't be here tonight."

"This is ridiculous! I cannot wait until this is over. The stress is becoming too much."

Emily rolled her eyes. "Get over yourself, Penny. People are going to begin accusing you soon because of your neuroticism."

Penelope's teacup clattered onto the saucer below. She glanced down at her dress with a rueful stare. "Now look what you've done!" she shouted, as she set the cup and saucer down and fled from the room to tend to the stain.

"Wow," Kelly said as Jodi slid the panel closed.

"Yeah, no kidding."

"She's guilty."

"She certainly acts it. Why else would she be so nervous?"

"Won't she be surprised that we've figured it out? We'll see who they call dim-witted then!" Kelly waved her fist in the air as they continued through the passage, veering right at the turn, and descending down the wobbly staircase.

They exited into the garden room and peered around the space. The room appeared empty.

Kelly scanned the space again. "Come on, let's go find someone."

"Well, not just anyone. We need to find someone who will listen to us. Like Abby or Willow."

"We can't wander around searching for Abby or Willow only."

Jodi arched her eyebrows. "Well, if we run into Melissa's goons, we're toast, so we'd better be careful."

Kelly waved her hand at her sister. "Okay, fine. We'll sneak around and try to avoid any unfriendlies."

Jodi's features curled in amusement. "Unfriendlies?"

"Yeah, like the people who hate us."

"It just sounded weird. Like we're in a war movie."

"We may as well be, the way these people are acting."

Kelly skirted around the bush hiding them and wound through the rose bushes in the room. They reached the door to the hallway. Jodi inched it open, and Kelly peered up and down the hall.

"Clear," Kelly whispered.

"No bogies?" Jodi inquired.

"No, Jodi," Kelly snarked, "no bogies on our six."

"Our six is behind us. They'd be at our nine or our three."

"Well, there are none there either, okay?"

"Just checking, since you wanted to go Full Metal Jacket."

"I don't even know what that means," Kelly said.

"The movie."

Kelly shrugged her shoulders as they slipped into the hall, heading toward the library. "I never saw it."

"Really? How did you never see it?"

"I don't watch that stuff."

"Oh, but you knew to call them unfriendlies?"

"Everyone knows that."

Jodi opened her mouth to protest, but Kelly waved her hand in the air to hush her. "Voices!" she whispered.

"Friendlies or unfriendlies?" Jodi breathed.

"Unfriendlies!" Kelly said, with a startled expression. "Run!"

CHAPTER 20

They spun in the opposite direction and raced down the hall. As they neared the corner, a shout erupted behind them.

"Faster!" Kelly urged.

"Hey, stop!" Madison shouted from behind them.

Kelly and Jodi whipped around the corner and ran headlong into the steppingstone hallway. They hopped from stone to stone as fast as they could.

"Into the carousel room!" Jodi shouted.

"We'll be trapped!"

"Hopefully they won't see us."

Kelly nodded as she hopped to dry land. She raced to the door and tugged it open, glancing over her shoulder as Jodi hopped onto the floor and joined her.

The door creaked open, and Jodi darted inside. Kelly slipped through the small opening and tugged the door shut behind her.

With the doors closed, the mechanism for the merry-go-round failed to start. Jodi toggled on her flashlight to cut through the blackness.

"Wow, it's creepy in here," Kelly whispered. She stared at the darkened lumps around the room. In the light, the horses didn't appear quite as frightening as in the meager light from Jodi's cell phone. In that light, they looked almost sinister.

"Did they see us, do you think?"

"No, we made it inside before they reached the corner."

"Good."

"Turn off the light," Kelly said, as a shout sounded down the hall.

Moments later, footsteps rushed past their location.

"–did they go?"

"I don't know. I thought they rounded the corner, but maybe they ducked–"

The voices trailed off as they swept past them on a search for the two of them.

"We should sneak out and go back the way we came while they search for us," Kelly said.

"Shouldn't we wait until they stop searching for us?"

"We could be in here all night!" Kelly said. "Plus, we know they went past that way." She pointed in the direction they'd been running before they slipped into the carousel room.

"We're going to have to room hop to avoid them until we run into someone who will listen to us."

"I hope we don't run into the ones who won't listen first," Kelly lamented as she put her hand on the large door handle.

"You're the one who wants to go!"

"We have to! We can't keep hiding! Okay, now, out and to the right as fast as you can and into the first doors we find."

Jodi shoved her cell phone into her pocket as Kelly inched the doors open. The floor chugged under their feet, trying to start, but failing as the doors were not open far enough.

"Clear!" Kelly said. She slid between the massive doors and into the hall with Jodi on her heels. They hopped onto the steppingstones, making it halfway through the stream, before they heard a shout at the end of the hall.

"Got 'em," Madison shouted down the hall.

"Eek!" Kelly shrieked. "Go back!" She swiveled around on her stone, intending to return the way they'd come moments earlier. Jodi, a stone behind her, failed to move.

"Go!" Kelly shouted.

When Jodi didn't move, Kelly glanced around her, finding Aurora racing toward them. She closed the distance to the stream.

"We're trapped," Jodi lamented.

"Like rats," Kelly said.

She glanced behind her. Madison had started to pick her way across the steppingstones toward them. She flailed her arms as she attempted to step from stone to stone in her heels.

"Get ready to run the way we were going," Kelly said under her breath to Jodi.

Jodi nodded, keeping her eyes trained on Aurora.

As Madison approached, Kelly jumped a stone closer to her. She reached out and shoved the woman as she hopped closer. On the wet, slippery stones, she struggled to keep her balance.

"Help!" she shouted to Aurora. Aurora's eyes went wide, and she stepped onto a stone. With as much speed as she could muster, Jodi hopped toward her and shoved her, too.

Both women toppled into the cold, flowing water. Shrieks filled the air as Kelly and Jodi hopscotched over the remaining stones and fled around the corner.

They raced through a set of double doors and into a darkened space. The scent of chlorine filled the air and light filtered from skylights above.

"A pool!" Kelly exclaimed.

"This room was locked before," Jodi said.

"Someone must have wanted to swim."

A noise sounded outside the room. "Hide!" Jodi breathed.

"Quick, in here!" Kelly shouted. They ducked through a windowless doorway and shoved it shut.

"Oh, great," Jodi bemoaned, as she toggled on her flashlight. "It's a sauna."

"Whew," Kelly breathed. "It's hot in here."

"I hope they don't take long to check out the pool. I'll die in this thing."

Kelly fanned herself. "Maybe we should hide behind one of these benches."

"Good idea."

They skirted around the cedar bench and ducked down behind it. Jodi doused her light.

After a few moments, Kelly groaned. "It's even hotter back here."

"I'm sweating."

"Me too!"

The door popped open, and lights flickered to life overhead. Kelly winced, squeezing her eyes shut as though it would make her invisible.

The door began to ease shut and they heard Aurora's voice call, "Clear!"

Kelly blew out the breath she'd been holding.

"Let's go," Jodi said.

"Wait! They could still be in the pool room. We should wait a few minutes."

"I hope I can last that long."

"You and me both. It's hotter than Hades in here." Kelly sat up and fanned herself again.

"If we inherit this place, I'm never using this room."

"Me either. I feel like my lungs are going to explode with this hot air. Who would want to sit in here and roast to death like a peanut?"

"Peanuts aren't alive."

"You know what I mean," Kelly said. "I feel like I'm a pig being roasted on a spit."

They waited a few more moments. "I can't take any more," Jodi said. "I have to get out of here."

"Let's listen at the door."

Kelly tiptoed across the room and pressed her ear against the hot cedar slabs decorating the door. After a listen, she inched the door open a crack. "Looks clear."

Jodi yanked the door out of her hands and burst into the room beyond. She gulped in air as she doubled over. Kelly followed after her, collapsing onto a chaise and covering her face.

"Whew," she said, blowing out a long breath.

"Worst hiding place ever."

"Okay, next time the crazies come after us, I'll let you pick the hiding spot."

"It's not going to be a sauna."

"No kidding," Kelly answered. "We already found the sauna. Unless they have two."

"Come on, let's keep going," Jodi said, wiping a bead of sweat from her brow and tugging at her shirt to cool off.

They crept to the doors and peeked into the hall. Kelly eased it shut, shaking her head. She signaled the number two with her fingers and pointed.

"Huh?" Jodi questioned.

Kelly puckered her lips and shook her head. "The two harpies are down the hall."

"Ohhhh," Jodi said, with a nod.

"What else would I have meant?"

"I don't know. Run to the second door?"

"That's the worst signal for 'run to the second door' ever."

"Oh, how would you do it then?"

"Like this." Kelly flipped her hand over, toggling her two

first fingers back and forth to indicate running, then flashed a two sign. "That's run to the second door."

"Whatever," Jodi said. "See if they're gone."

Kelly glanced into the hallway. She nodded. "Gone," she mouthed. "Let's go. Across the hall and down to the first door."

Jodi nodded and they hurried out of the pool room, making a diagonal line across the hall to the next room. They ducked inside the billiards room, pressing the doors closed behind them. Kelly leaned her back against them and squeezed her eyes shut.

The cracking of two billiards balls caused her to snap them open again. She stared wide-eyed into the room. Aubrey rose to stand from her crouch over the table, pool cue in hand.

CHAPTER 21

"Aubrey!" Kelly shouted, grabbing hold of Jodi's arm and squeezing.

Aubrey leaned against her stick and narrowed her eyes at them. "The whole house is looking for you two."

"I know!" Kelly insisted.

"One shout and you're caught."

"Please don't," Kelly said.

"Why not?"

"We didn't do anything wrong! We didn't kill Pearl or Melissa!"

"Says you. Everyone else thinks you did it."

"That's not true," Jodi said. "Your mother doesn't think we did it."

"How would you know that?"

"We overheard her earlier," Kelly explained.

"Oh, so you were eavesdropping?"

"Yes."

"Interesting."

"We're eavesdroppers, not murderers," Kelly said. "There's a huge difference."

Voices sounded in the hall again. Kelly shot Aubrey a pleading glance.

"Get behind the curtains," she answered.

"Thanks."

Kelly and Jodi hurried across the room and hid behind the thick red velvet drapes. Aubrey leaned over the pool table, hitting another ball into a side pocket. The door popped open. Kelly barely heard what was said over the blood rushing through her ears.

Aubrey didn't answer for a moment, instead lining up another shot and cracking the white ball into a purple striped ball. She stood and chalked her cue before she glanced at the door. "I haven't seen them.

The door closed and Kelly blew out a breath. "You're welcome," Aubrey answered.

"Thanks," Kelly said, as she stepped from behind the curtain.

"This doesn't mean I think you're innocent, you know."

Kelly's shoulders slumped. "We didn't do it."

"But we think we know who did," Jodi said.

"Really?" Aubrey questioned.

"Yes."

"Who?"

"Penelope," Kelly and Jodi said at the same time.

Aubrey's forehead crinkled. "Seriously? You think Penelope killed Pearl and Melissa?"

"Yes," Kelly said again. "We went through all the information, and she's the one who would stand to gain."

Aubrey shook her head and returned to her pool game. "Whatever. Good luck with proving that."

"Have you seen Willow or Abby?" Kelly inquired.

"Nope."

Kelly sighed.

"I guess we should move on," Jodi suggested.

Kelly nodded. "Okay."

"Good luck!" Aubrey called as they strode to the door.

Kelly held back rolling her eyes at the unhelpful comment. After a glance into the hall, they slipped out and around the corner. They pushed into the library, coming face to face with Peyton.

She arched her eyebrows high at them. "Well, well, well, if it isn't the two most popular women in the house."

"We can explain," Kelly said, holding her hands out in front of her.

"Save it," Peyton answered.

"No, really, we can— "Jodi started, when Peyton interrupted her.

"I couldn't really care less."

"But we didn't do it!" Kelly shouted.

"Maybe you did and maybe you didn't, but I don't really care. I just want to get out of this house."

Peyton pushed between them and threw open the doors, wandering into the hall.

Kelly heard a shout from down the hall as she shoved the doors closed.

"Have you seen—"

"Nope," Peyton interrupted, and continued her saunter down the hall.

"Why won't anyone help us?" Kelly huffed.

"I'll help you," a voice piped up from a wing-backed chair near the fireplace. Kelly and Jodi snapped their heads toward the voice. Julia rose from the chair and eyed them.

"Julia," Kelly said. "Thank goodness someone is willing to help us. We didn't do this!"

"Who did?" she asked.

"We think it was Penelope," Kelly answered.

Julia cocked her head at the statement. "She's nervous and

she stood to gain if Pearl and Melissa were out of the way. And she's determined to pin it on Willow."

"Why would she point the finger at someone else like that unless she was guilty?" Jodi added.

"Maybe because she thinks Willow is guilty."

"Either way, it's not us. You have to help us convince Melissa's friends. They're literally hunting us down and we're innocent!"

Julia considered it before she spoke. "All right. I'll help you."

Kelly breathed out a sigh of relief. "Thank you."

"Wait here," Julia said.

Kelly nodded as she skirted past them and out the door.

"Do you think we can trust her?" Jodi asked.

"Gosh, I hope so, because I'm getting sick and tired of this." She sank into the armchair and let her chin fall into her palm.

Jodi joined her. They waited for a few minutes, before Kelly leapt up from her chair and paced the floor. "Where did she go for help? The moon?"

"It's only been a few minutes," Jodi said.

"Seems like it's been an hour."

She paced around in front of the fireplace for another few moments before the doors opened. Julia appeared and Kelly smiled at her.

"We were starting to wonder if you—" Her voice cut off as she spotted who trailed behind her. Harper strode into the room with her eyes narrowed and a cat-who-caught-the-canary expression plastered on her features.

"Harper!" Kelly exclaimed.

Jodi vaulted from her seat, stunned.

"I'll leave you ladies to, ah, talk," Julia said with a coy smile, as she spun on her heel and strode from the room.

"Well, well, well," Harper said, "look who it is."

"Now, Harper, just listen," Kelly began.

"Listen to what? Your confession?"

"No!" Jodi shouted. "We're innocent!"

"So you say!" Harper shouted back, stamping her foot on the floor.

"Think about it!" Kelly yelled. "Why would we kill Pearl or Melissa?"

"Money," Harper said, crossing her arms over her chest.

"How would we know we were getting money? No one knew!"

"You could have overheard details of the will."

"Where? In the five-star restaurant we can't afford to eat at? Or maybe at the boutique clothing store we can't afford to shop in?" Kelly said.

"You're the one who has been making fun of our knock-off clothes. We'd never be anywhere in common with Pearl," Jodi added.

"Maybe you work there and overheard it."

"I work at Pearls Unlimited," Kelly said. "And the Hallmark store. So, unless Pearl has been doing some card shopping, I wouldn't have been in contact with her."

Harper turned her attention to Jodi. "What about you?"

"I work at a craft store. Has Pearl recently been knitting?"

Harper set her jaw; her eyes still narrowed at them. "Still—"

"Still nothing!" Kelly shouted. "It makes no sense. Accusing us makes *no* sense."

"Then who did it?"

"We think we have an idea," Kelly said.

"Oh, really? How do I know you're not going to just accuse someone to get the suspicion off you?"

"Because we have reasons, okay? We've listed everyone out and gone over their motives and everything."

"Okay, so who did it?"

"Penelope," Jodi said.

"Melissa's cousin?"

Kelly nodded.

"Why would Penelope kill her aunt and her cousin?"

"Because in the original will, the one where Melissa inherited everything, Penelope was the only Barlow who stood to gain if Pearl and Melissa died. She was named along with Parker and Addison."

"And it sounds like, from what we've overheard," Jodi added, "that the Barlows are none too happy that they were basically cut out of the will, since it was Mr. Barlow's money that saved the Willow estate."

Kelly nodded. "And Pearl took it and gave everything to Melissa. In the event of her death, it went to the cousins. Everyone except Willow."

"How do you know Willow didn't do it out of anger for being left out of the will?"

"Because she said she doesn't want anything from Pearl after what happened with her mother, and if she was angry about being left out of the will, what does killing the woman do to solve that?"

"Gets rid of her anger?"

"But means she's penniless anyway."

Harper stared at them for a moment. "Why would Penelope kill Melissa?"

"Does she inherit if Melissa is dead? We don't know what Melissa's will says, but maybe she inherits part of the estate if both women are dead."

"Except you two are inheriting the estate."

"But no one knew that, duh," Kelly said.

Harper clenched her jaw and mulled it over. She lifted her chin and stared at them. "No, I don't believe you. I'm going to tell everyone where you are, and the police can arrest you when they get here."

She spun on her heel and stalked to the door.

"No!" Kelly shouted, rushing forward.

Harper pulled the doors shut before Kelly could reach them. The sound of a lock clicking outside sealed their fate. Kelly spun the knobs but to no avail. They were locked inside the library, and Harper was rounding up a posse to deal with them.

"What now?" she asked Jodi.

Jodi rubbed the back of her neck as she shrugged. "I don't know. Try to talk reason into them when they get here?"

"Oh, yeah, because that went so well with Harper." Kelly scanned the room. "Come on, help me search for a secret passage."

"Seriously?"

"Yes! Maybe there's a way out and we can sneak away. There's no way I want to be here when Harper gets back!"

"Okay," Jodi said.

They spread out across the room and started to search the room for triggers to a secret passage. Kelly tugged on a wall sconce to no avail when she heard the lock click. Her eyes widened and she backed toward Jodi as the door slowly opened.

Grabbing Jodi's hand, she squeezed her eyes shut, expecting Harper and her harpies to pile into the room with pitchforks and torches. When she pried one eye open, she found Everly easing the doors shut. The woman held a finger to her lips.

Kelly's brow furrowed.

Everly held her hands in front of her as she explained. "I overheard Harper telling Aurora and Maddie about what you told her."

"Are you here to lock us in the dungeon?" Kelly asked.

"No. I believe you! I'm here to help you. We need to make sure Penelope pays for this!"

Kelly and Jodi breathed a collective sigh of relief. "Oh, thank heavens," Kelly said, pressing her palm to her chest. "Finally, someone believes us. We didn't do this!"

"But we think Penelope did," Jodi said.

"Tell me what you know," Everly answered.

Her eyes fell to the photo peeking from Kelly's cardigan pocket, as Kelly yammered through their theory. "Okay, everyone here was working from the premise that Pearl didn't change her will. The original will— "

"– which we have a copy of–" Jodi added.

"– gave everything to Melissa," Kelly said.

"But if Melissa was dead, the estate was divided between Penelope, Addison, and Parker."

"So, we started to think of who would benefit if both Pearl and Melissa were dead."

Jodi continued, "And we figured it was one of the three nieces."

"After we ruled out Willow, since she was left out of the will."

Jodi nodded and continued with the explanation. "Out of those three, the ones most angry with Pearl—"

"And probably Melissa," Kelly added.

"Were the Barlows."

"Of which Penelope is one."

"So, she's the most likely culprit," Jodi finished.

"We're just waiting on confirmation that she benefits from Melissa's will, and then we'll have all the information we need."

"You don't have a copy of Melissa's will?"

"No," Kelly said. "It was in the office and now it's missing."

"But you've seen a copy of it and know what's in it?"

"No, I found it earlier but didn't look at it," Jodi replied.

"Abby's checking on it for us," Kelly said. Her phone chimed. "Oh, maybe that's her now."

Kelly glanced at her phone. A message from Abby showed on her screen. Her brows wrinkled as she read it and she swallowed hard. Her stomach turned over and her palms turned sweaty. She read the message a second time to be sure of what it said. But there it was, in black text framed in a bright blue bubble. *Melissa's will names Everly Dixon as her sole heir. Weird, I can't figure out why? Meet to discuss?*

She licked her lips as she shoved the phone into her pocket.

"Was it her?" Everly questioned.

"Yeah," Kelly said.

"What did she say?" Jodi asked.

"Nothing. Uh, she hasn't found anything yet. Told us to sit tight." Kelly pulled her lips into a line. "Well, I guess we'll just do that then. Maybe best to do that in our room, though, before Harper gets back."

Kelly grabbed Jodi's arm and tugged her toward Everly, who stood between them and the door.

"Thanks for your help," she said.

"Sorry," Everly answered before they reached the door. "I can't let you leave."

Kelly glanced up to argue, finding the business end of a handgun pointed at them. Everly's face had turned cold, her features settling into a scowl.

CHAPTER 22

Kelly held up her hands. "Look, Everly–"

"Don't even try it," Everly barked. "I'm sure Abby already spilled the beans."

"Spilled what beans?" Kelly questioned.

Everly waved them back toward the fireplace. Kelly swallowed hard as she and Jodi backed away from the gun-wielding woman.

"You know I'm Melissa's heir," she answered.

Jodi glanced at Kelly, shock on her face. "Well, I didn't know! You could have let me go."

"Hey! Thanks a lot, Jodi!"

Jodi rolled her eyes and murmured through a tightened jaw, "I could have gone for help!'

"Yeah, and left me to die. Real nice."

"That's enough!" Everly shouted.

"Is it? Are you going for four murders in one weekend?" Kelly questioned, suddenly emboldened. "You'll never get away with it."

"I might."

"Are you going to pin this one on Willow? She'd have no reason to kill us."

"No, but Harper would. Or Maddie, or Aurora. They've been out for blood all weekend. Maybe things got out of hand when they confronted you about killing Pearl and Melissa."

"That'll never work."

"You'd be surprised what I can make work."

Kelly swallowed hard. "Why?"

"What?" Everly barked.

"Why did you do it? Why kill Pearl? And Melissa?"

"To get what's mine," Everly said, through clenched teeth.

"Their money?" Kelly questioned.

"How do you figure it's yours?" Jodi added.

Everly's gaze fell to Kelly's pocket. She wiggled the gun at the picture peeking out. Kelly followed her focus. She pulled the picture out.

"This is you," she said. "Willow told us."

Everly nodded. "Yep."

"It was mixed in with pictures of Melissa as a kid," Kelly recalled aloud.

"Why?" Jodi asked.

"We grew up together."

"Still, why would they have this picture of you in with their daughter?"

Everly narrowed her eyes and shook her head. "I was always here – always with Melissa, always hiding in her shadow."

"Were you just jealous of her? None of this is yours. You weren't a Barlow."

"That's where you're wrong," Everly said.

Kelly frowned in thought.

Everly cocked her head. "I am a Barlow."

"What?" Kelly asked.

"That's right. Melissa and I were sisters. Well, half-sisters. I was born a few months after her. My father was Philip Barlow, and my mother was Marlene Dixon, his mistress."

"Ohhhhhh," Kelly said, as realization dawned on her. "And he brought you here to see you grow up."

"But you were always on the outside. So close to all that wealth, but never able to get it," Jodi said.

"Until now. Now, who's having the last laugh." Thunder punctuated her statement.

"So you killed Pearl and then Melissa to steal their money?" Kelly said, shaking her head.

"Their money? That was my father's money. He dumped all he had into this place." She waved the gun around wildly. "And when he died he left everything to Pearl. She gave me nothing. Didn't even want to see me. She got what she deserved."

"But you killed your sister!"

"The little snip deserved it, too."

"How can you say that? You must have been friends. You were college roommates!"

"That was by design of my father. She had no idea we were half-sisters. Not until a few months ago." Everly stalked back and forth across the room as she chuckled. "That blew her mind, let me tell you."

"You told her? What did she say?" Kelly glanced around the room in search of a weapon she may be able to grab.

"She told me she didn't care. Called me all kinds of names. Said she was her daddy's choice and his heir. She said if he really wanted to claim me, he should have put me in his will."

"How did you convince her to put you in hers?" Jodi asked.

"I threatened to expose daddy's little indiscretion to the world. Pearl nearly flipped her lid. She did *not* want Philip

Barlow's bastard coming to light. It would make her look weak, she said. Ruin her. I didn't care.

"Melissa finally promised me her inheritance. I told her that would do for now. And I had to be welcomed back into the fold until the old lady kicked it."

Kelly shook her head. "And then you planned to kill them."

Everly shrugged in agreement. "I figured, what better way than at this ridiculous party? First Pearl, then Melissa. Pin it on you two and get away with it and all the money, too!" Everly shot them a shocked face. "Me? I was named in the will?"

"But that didn't quite work out, did it?" Jodi said.

Everly narrowed her eyes at them, ceasing her ambling back and forth. "No. No one knew Pearl made the little switcheroo on her will, apparently not even Melissa."

"But it'll never stand. Giving all this to two strangers? It'll never hold up in court. All I need to do is wait for Addy, Parker, and Penny to sue, and the original will goes back into effect. And I end up taking it all."

She tossed her head back and let out a harsh cackle. "Now all I need to do is end the two of you, and I'll be scot-free." She leveled her weapon.

"No, please. We won't say anything. In fact, we'll help you. We'll refuse the inheritance. Sign it all over to you," Kelly pleaded.

"Yeah, I'll bet," Everly barked.

"I promise! We never wanted any of this!"

"Enough!" Everly shouted. "The answer is no. Now, which one of you first?"

A tear spilled onto Kelly's cheek as she gripped Jodi's hands and squeezed. "I love you, Jodi."

"I love you, Kelly," Jodi cried.

Kelly squeezed her eyes shut as she waited for the bullet

to strike her. She squashed her lips together until they hurt. Her heart pounded in her chest and her knees felt weak. Thunder boomed overhead and she jumped in place as a loud *thunk* sounded after it. She waited. She didn't feel any pain. Her lower lip trembled as she wondered if Everly had shot Jodi first. She felt the warmth of Jodi's hand still pressed against hers.

Kelly pulled her eyes open to slits and glanced sideways. Jodi still stood with her eyes squeezed shut, gulping in breaths, her lips pulled into a frightened wince. She glanced at Everly. Her eyes widened and she patted Jodi's arm.

"Jodi! Jodi, look!"

Jodi opened her eyes and they both stared at the scene ahead. Willow stood in front of the open door, a fireplace poker clutched in her hand. Everly lay sprawled on the floor, her eyes closed, and a pained expression on her face.

Kelly rushed forward, kicking the gun away from the woman's hand. Jodi pulled a tissue from her pocket and used it to gingerly pick up the weapon.

"Thank you," Kelly said to Willow.

"No problem. I heard shouting coming from in here. I heard her confess. I grabbed the first thing I could find and hurried back here to help you."

"You probably saved our lives," Jodi said.

"You didn't deserve what was happening to you," Willow answered. "And now the right person will pay for these crimes."

Moments later, Harper, Madison, Abby, Julia, and Aurora raced into the room. They scanned the scene, eyes wide.

"Here's the guilty party. I heard her confess," Willow said, motioning to Everly, who groaned on the floor.

"We just figured that out when Abby told us about the will," Julia said.

Abby nodded. "After I didn't hear from you, I went to

Julia. I ran into Harper along the way. I explained everything, and we were on our way to find you and look for Everly to sort this out."

"She was Philip Barlow's daughter," Willow explained. "And she wanted what she thought was hers."

Harper glanced down at her, her nose wrinkling with disdain. "And she killed Melissa to get it."

Everly's eyes fluttered open, and she glanced around. "Harper! There they are! Get them!"

"It's over, Everly," Harper spat out.

"We should lock her in the pantry until the police arrive!" Aurora shouted.

Madison nodded. "Get her, ladies!" Harper ordered.

"Wait! You've got it all wrong, Harper!" Everly tried.

"Save it for the judge," Harper hollered, as they led her down the hall.

Julia turned to Kelly and Jodi. "I am so sorry about all of this."

"No problem," Kelly said. "I'm just glad we got it sorted out."

"Me too," Jodi agreed.

Julia nodded. "Kennedy spoke with the police. With any luck, they'll be here within the hour."

"But how with the storm?" Kelly questioned.

"They've arranged a boat."

"Better late than never, I guess."

Kennedy entered the room, her phone in her hand. "Oh, good, you found them."

"Just in time," Willow said. "They were nearly blown away by the real guilty party."

"The police should be here soon. They can handle her." She turned to Kelly and Jodi. "In the meantime, there's something we need to discuss. If you'll follow me."

Kelly flicked her gaze to Jodi then back to Kennedy and

nodded. This must be the part where she'd let them down gently, tell them they'd never actually inherit the estate. She wasn't surprised, though she couldn't help but feel a little let down. It had been nice imagining owning a house like this, even with all its stairs; never having to worry about paying your bills from month to month, enjoying the high life.

Sadly, though, Kelly ruminated as they followed Kennedy from the room, it was not to be. It was fun while it lasted though.

EPILOGUE

SIX MONTHS LATER

Kelly wrestled with a box stuffed in the backseat of her small car. Wedged between the front seat and the door opening, she tugged at it to try to free it from the car.

"Why did I put so much in this one?" she lamented aloud to herself.

After another full minute of yanking and pulling, angling, and shifting, the box gave way. With the corners of her lips turning upward, Kelly wrangled it free and lifted it up. Her smile turned to a frown as a random assortment of items pounded to the ground around her feet, scattering in every direction.

"Nice to see some things haven't changed," Jodi shouted, as she strolled over.

"Nope," Kelly said, as she tried to rebuild the box and collect the wayward items. "My luck hasn't changed."

Jodi grabbed the remaining items and tossed them into the questionable container. Kelly slid her arm underneath as she lifted it in an attempt to keep the bottom from giving way again. She rose to stand with Jodi and stared upward.

The massive sprawling structure of Willow Lake Manor loomed over them.

"I still can't believe we actually did inherit this place," Kelly said.

"Maybe your luck has actually changed," Jodi said, as she eyed the huge house.

"I'm not sure about that. We inherited a house where two people were murdered. I really hope it's not haunted."

"If it is, think of the haunted hotel income we could make."

"I'd rather it's not."

"Then I'm sure we can have some killer murder mystery parties. The ambiance is built-in!"

"Don't say killer parties. You said that before this one and look what happened. It came true!"

Jodi chuckled. "How many more murders can one person witness in a lifetime?"

"Don't ask. I don't want to find out."

"Come on," Jodi said, clapping her hand on Kelly's shoulder. "I'll race you to the carousel."

"Hey!" Kelly shouted, as Jodi scurried into the house. "No fair, I have a huge box!" She hurried after her. "We really need to have a conversation about this weeping lady fountain! It's super creepy!"

"Last one to the merry-go-round's a rotten egg!" Jodi called over her shoulder.

Kelly shook her head at her sister as her eyes floated around the massive foyer. Her lips turned upward into a smile again.

Their new life was going to be quite the adventure.

* * *

Keep reading with *Mayhem in the Mansion,* book 2 in the Pearl Party Cozy Mysteries!

A NOTE FROM THE AUTHOR

Dear Reader,

Thank you for reading this book! *Murder of Pearl* is based off of real pearl parties and their hosts.

I hope you enjoyed reading this book as much as I did writing it! If you loved it, please consider leaving a review and help get the book into the hands of other interested readers.

Book 2 in this series isn't available yet, but look for it coming in 2023! In the meantime, if you love cozy mysteries, try *Ghosts, Lore & a House by the Shore*, available now!

If you'd like to stay up to date with all my news, be the first to find out about new releases first, sales and get free offers, join the Nellie H. Steele's Mystery Readers' Group! Or sign up for my newsletter now!

All the best, Nellie

OTHER SERIES BY NELLIE H. STEELE

Cozy Mystery Series

Cate Kensie Mysteries
Lily & Cassie by the Sea Mysteries
Pearl Party Mysteries
Middle Age is Murder Cozy Mysteries

Supernatural Suspense/Urban Fantasy

Shadow Slayers Stories
Duchess of Blackmoore Mysteries
Shelving Magic

Adventure

Maggie Edwards Adventures
Clif & Ri on the Sea

www.ingramcontent.com/pod-product-compliance
Lightning Source LLC
Chambersburg PA
CBHW070504200726
48293CB00007B/2369